# *Butterfly Girl*

## SARAH FLOYD

Butterfly Girl



Summary: Twelve-year-old Meghan is abandoned on her grandfather's Oregon farm, stumbles on an ancestor's magic spell book…and sprouts wings. When her absentee-mother shows up with superstar plans for her Winged Wonder Girl, Meghan must decide if a Hollywood life with the mother she longed for is worth leaving the friends who stood by her, and Grandpa, who loved her before the whole world knew her name.

ISBN: 978-1-964885-05-6

Republished by:
Wild Ink Publishing
Camp Hill, Pennsylvania
www.wild-ink-publishing.com

*With love and thanks to my wingmen,*
*Doug and Daniel*

# Contents

# Butterfly Girl

# Not Fair at the Fair

MEGHAN PICKED A marigold and snapped the stem short. She turned to her grandfather and stuck the golden-orange blossom in his button hole. "You look handsome, Grandpa," she said.

"Thank you, darlin'." He grinned and bent at the waist in a courtly bow. "Got to make a good impression on the judges."

Meghan followed Grandpa past the tool shed to the old white truck. She yanked hard to unstick the rusty passenger-side door. He was already revving the engine, the sound muffled in the morning fog that clung to the hills. They bumped down the dirt and gravel road, tires churning up dust, then turned onto the blacktop that led to the highway. Dewy fields and orchards sped by, row after row, mile after mile, the colors and patterns flowing together in a blur.

Meghan rolled down the window and squinted her eyes against the rushing wind. Her hair whipped around—it almost felt like she was flying. She'd whoosh right out the window and up into the air, soaring high into the blue sky, the cool wind under her wings. She smiled to herself. *Arms.* The cool wind under her arms.

Grandpa glanced at her. "You feeling sick? Want me to pull over?"

Loose papers began blowing around inside the truck. Meghan rolled the window closed. "I'm okay. Just getting some fresh air." She rummaged in her backpack and pulled out a hairbrush, worked through the tangles, and began weaving a pencil-thin braid in her honey-brown hair. She tied it off with a rubber band and started a new one next to it.

"Is hippy back in style?" The corners of his eyes crinkled in a smile.

"Grandpa! It's *retro*, not hippy." Ten minutes later, Meghan spotted the giant Ferris wheel and then the zipper ride, carousel, and midway games, with exhibition halls and horse corrals near the entrance. A red, white, and blue banner fluttered in the breeze: *Oregon State Fair.*

••

A FTER THEY PARKED and checked in with the organizers, Grandpa headed back to the truck. "You're in charge of the strawberries." He handed Meghan a small cardboard box and grabbed a larger one for himself. They joined the crowd that streamed toward the entrance of the exhibition hall.

"We're in the last row," Grandpa said. He led the way, winding through the aisles, passing farmers busily arranging displays of fruits and vegetables. "This is it. Number ninety-seven."

Meghan set her box on the table. "I'm going up front to look for Jade." Jade had been her best friend ever since the day they met at the sandbox in the park, back when Meghan lived in town with her mom and dad.

Grandpa shook his head. "Slow down, now. Don't go running off."

"But Grandpa—you promised. You said when I turned twelve I could walk around on my own."

"What? You don't want to hang out here with your old grandpa?" He pressed his hand to his heart.

"That's not what I meant Grandpa, it's just…"

He winked at her. "You can go around by yourself, as soon as your friend shows up."

A leathery-skinned farmer lifted his chin in greeting from a few tables away. "Morning, Mike. You going to let someone else win this year?"

"Top of the morning to you!" Grandpa smiled. "That's a good-looking basket you got there, no telling who'll win."

Grandpa reached into his box and pulled out a quilted yellow banner. "Grandma's banner always brings us luck," he said, and unfolded the wide swath of fabric. Green letters spelled out *The Real McCoy Organic Acres,* with strawberries, carrots, and clover embroidered along the border. Her grandmother had made it before she died, back when Meghan was still a baby. Meghan draped the banner across the table and smoothed the edges.

Grandpa set out a faded wicker basket and soon he and Meghan had it overflowing with baseball-sized tomatoes, plump golden corn, and shiny red strawberries the size of a baby's fist.

One by one, farmers stopped by to admire his basket. Before long a crowd had gathered in a semicircle around the table.

Someone asked, "Where do you buy your manure?" Others wanted to know about seed quality and planting rotations, each one trying to figure out how Grandpa's land produced such an amazing crop.

"Hey, McCoy," said a wrinkled old farmer, "can you spare a little leprechaun dust? That land of yours is rockier than mine!" Meghan smiled. *Leprechaun dust.* Grandpa mixed chicken poop with cow manure, sometimes he added oak ashes and compost. His secret formula.

Grandpa laughed and put on his thickest Irish accent. "Maybe it's magic or maybe it's luck. One thing's for sure— it's a lot of work!" The other farmers chuckled along with him. Mike McCoy was hardworking and honest. No one could begrudge him a win.

"Jade!" Meghan called, spotting her friend's dark hair ducking through the crowd. "Over here!"

Jade wove her way up to their table and smiled at Grandpa. "My mom said to tell you 'Hi,' and she hopes you win!"

"Thank your mom for me, okay?" he said, smiling back at her. He gestured toward the exhibition hall's open doors. "You girls have fun, now. The judging is at twelve o'clock. Maybe I'll take a ride with you on the Ferris wheel after that."

••

"What do you want to do first?" Jade asked.

"We could check out the calves—they're adorable, and we can see if the horse competitions are starting soon too." Meghan pushed her dollars deep into her pocket. "I don't have much money and it has to last all day."

Jade groaned as the horse arena came into view. "I guess you-know-who had the same idea." A tall girl with copper-red hair lounged against the side of the corral, watching a rider warm up in the ring. Greta Von Stratton—surrounded by other fashionably dressed girls, as usual.

"Quick! Let's go look at the calves." Meghan grabbed Jade's elbow. "Maybe she didn't see us."

"Too late," Jade muttered, her teeth clenched tight.

"Well, look who's here." Greta strolled across the dusty ground in expensive leather boots. Faded designer jeans, an "old" t-shirt that probably cost a mint, and a soft suede cowboy hat finished the look.

Meghan glanced down at her tie-dyed shirt and favorite jeans, the knees threadbare from kneeling in the garden. "Hi Greta," she said, looking up to meet Greta's eyes.

Greta smiled. "I didn't know you were interested in horses. It's not like you actually own any."

Meghan's heart pounded, but she couldn't think of a snappy reply. Jade glared at Greta, but Meghan focused on the next rider entering the corral.

"My dad's foreman is showing one of our horses today," Greta said.

Meghan kept her eyes on the ring.

"Hey Greta!"

Meghan turned to see who it was. Her stomach did a quick tickly flip. Danny Taylor and two of his friends were walking toward them.

"Meghan!" he said. "I haven't seen you all summer." His friends drifted off and joined the girls at the side of the corral. Danny pushed the shaggy blond hair out of his eyes. "Where you been hiding?"

Their teacher had partnered Meghan and Danny for a social studies project last year. Danny was hardworking and smart. And nice. She smiled at him. "I've been helping my grandfather—right now it's just the two of us. But he'll hire some farmworkers during harvest season…"

Greta let out a loud sigh and said, "She had to help her dear old grandpappy out in the fields." She flicked her glossy hair off her shoulders. "I almost feel sorry for you, Meghan. What a boring summer. Work, work, work—just you and your grandpappy, all by your lonesome, plotting and scheming out there in the boonies."

Heat rushed to Meghan's face. "What? I don't even know what you're talking about."

Jade bumped against Meghan's side. "Let's get out of here."

"What is your problem?" Danny said, shaking his head at Greta.

Greta's eyes glinted like shards of green glass. "Did you ever wonder why they work *alone* so much of the time, and why their farm wins the blue ribbon *every single year*?"

She turned to Meghan. "You can drop the Little Miss Innocent act. You don't fool me."

Meghan stepped back like she'd been pushed. "You think my grandfather's cheating?" Compost, manure, and ashes were organic—totally legit. Not that she was going to tell Greta about Grandpa's secret formula.

Danny gave Greta a long look. "No one's a cheater. Maybe their farm gets more sun where they are, or something like that."

"Yeah, right. Sunshine." Greta adjusted the brim of her cowboy hat. "Or maybe her grandfather hasn't told her exactly what he's doing." She glanced at Meghan and shrugged her shoulders in what might have been a half-hearted apology.

"My grandfather would never cheat anybody." Meghan's voice shook a little.

"Whatever. Just forget about it. Don't start crying or anything."

"I'm not crying! But you have no right to talk about him that way."

"Okay, well…sorry." Greta rolled her eyes.

"Come on," Danny said, looking back and forth between Greta and Meghan. "Let's all do something—it's the fair." He smiled at Meghan.

Meghan tried to smile back at him. "Thanks, but we're going to hang out here for a while." It would be great to walk around with Danny, but she couldn't take another minute of Greta's snarky mouth.

"You sure?"

Meghan nodded.

Greta called out to her friends, "Let's ride some rides!" She linked arms with Danny, gazing at him through lashes thick with mascara. "I want to ride the Ferris wheel." Danny stumbled a little as she pulled him toward their friends at the side of the corral.

Soon it would be Greta and Danny, laughing and talking, the two of them alone on top of the Ferris wheel. Meghan watched him walk away. *Danny and Greta sittin' in a tree, K-I-S-S-I-N-G…*

"What was Greta yapping about?" Jade asked.

"When are you talking about? She did a lot of yapping."

"That thing she said about your grandpa cheating. Not that I think he ever would!"

Meghan shrugged. "Beats me. She's probably jealous because her dad's never won."

"I can't believe you and Greta were ever friends." Jade wrinkled her nose, like she smelled something bad.

"I was what, five? It's not like I really had a choice, our moms took us to that art class together. And anyway, back then Greta wasn't so, so—"

"So obnoxious? So stuck-up?" Jade grinned. "Oh, there are *so* many words I can think of to describe Greta."

Meghan laughed. "Too bad she couldn't stay five forever."

They paused to watch as Greta and Danny's group stopped at a frozen lemonade stand. While Danny was busy shoving his change into his pocket, Greta grabbed the lemonade cup off the counter. She dodged to the side, twirling around and swapping the cup from hand to hand, keeping it just out of his reach. Danny darted back and forth, laughing, and trying to grab the cup.

"What does he see in her?" Jade shook her head in disgust.

Meghan sighed. "She's always had a thing for him, maybe he's finally noticed." Meghan stared after Danny until the crowd engulfed him. He used to be shorter and kind of skinny. And now he'd let his hair grow out. He had definitely gotten cuter over the summer.

Meghan and Jade wandered through the animal pens. They reached through the slats to pet the wide-eyed, bewildered calves and scruffy baby goats, then stopped to watch a sheep shearing demonstration, the wool peeling off in one big, fluffy fleece, with a few small tufts drifting to the ground.

"Now I'm in the mood for cotton candy," Meghan said.

Jade nodded, licking her lips. "Me too, but let's go the other way so we don't run into Miss Snobby Pants. If she gets in my face again I might have to take her down. Somebody should wipe that smirk off her face." She whirled around, poised to attack an imaginary opponent. "Beware the wrath of Jade!"

Meghan laughed. "Better watch out, Greta!"

Jade performed a series of kicks, ending with a perfect roundhouse, eyes narrowed, hair spinning around her face like a shiny black halo. A few passersby stopped to watch her. Jade bowed. She was small, but her wiry muscles hinted at the years of practice that had earned her a brown belt in taekwondo. Jade's parents adopted her from Korea when she was a baby—martial arts was her thing. Her parents enrolled her in classes when she was four, a way to honor her heritage.

••

MEGHAN GLANCED AT her watch. "Uh oh, look at the time." It was eleven fifty-five. "Judging's at twelve."

They jogged toward the opposite side of the fairgrounds, weaving through the midway crowd to the narrow strip of grass behind the food vendors, where they could run. They were hot and breathless by the time they pushed against the double doors of the exhibition hall. A blast of icy air conditioning washed over them as they entered, goose bumping their arms.

"Looks like the judges already announced the winners," Meghan said, pointing to a second-place ribbon pinned to a basket on her left. They turned down Grandpa's row. Farmers and other spectators clustered around his table.

A large, red-faced man elbowed his way to the front of the crowd. It was Robert Von Stratton, Greta's father. "That's a mighty fine-looking basket, seeing as how you never used any chemicals." He was talking to Grandpa, but his voice boomed loud for everyone to hear.

"You got enough money, Von Stratton," an old farmer said. And it was true. Robert Von Stratton's organic farm was the biggest in the county. He didn't need the five hundred dollar prize for winning first place. "Why don't you leave the man be?"

Mr. Von Stratton ignored him and reached into Grandpa's basket. He picked up a giant strawberry, dangling it by the stem. The rich ruby color gleamed in the lights of the exhibition hall. "No sirree, no chemicals was needed to grow these beauties."

Meghan stood on tiptoes and strained to see past the people in front of her. Jade found a gap and dragged Meghan behind her. They could see Grandpa's face now, he was standing next to his basket—which had a first-place ribbon pinned to it.

His blue-gray eyes were locked on Mr. Von Stratton. "A man has a right to take care of his family," he said. "I've done nothing wrong." Aside from the cash prize, a farmer could advertise that his farm had won the blue ribbon— and that brought higher prices and new customers. "No chemicals have touched these crops."

Someone in the back yelled, "Sore loser!"

Mr. Von Stratton spun around. "Who said that?"

Dead silence. No one wanted to pick a fight with Robert Von Stratton—the man was the size of a pro linebacker. His gaze flickered from face to face. "If the man's won fair and square, then I got no bone to pick with him."

He waved the strawberry in front of a long-haired young farmer. "My strawberries don't look like this. How about yours?" He hefted an oversized pink-and-yellow striped tomato. "How about this little beauty?" He tossed the tomato and the strawberry toward the basket. The tomato bounced off an ear of corn and rolled onto the table. "Mighty strange if you ask me."

"I didn't hear anyone asking you," Grandpa said, and he pulled his basket closer. His neck flushed red, but his voice came out cool and steady. "If you're done talking, I'll thank you to keep your hands off my produce."

Mr. Von Stratton glared at him, then turned and stomped off, his steps pounding loud across the concrete floor.

"What was that all about?" Meghan asked, when she and Jade reached the table.

Grandpa glanced toward the exhibition hall's steel doors. "That man's not happy unless he's the center of attention—it's about the glory, not the money. Let's not let him steal our joy, okay?"

Grandpa nodded at the blue ribbon attached to his basket, with the words *Organic Medley Best of Show* written in gold letters across the center medallion. "You and me, darlin', we did it again." The corners of his eyes crinkled in a smile. "Now, how about a ride on the Ferris wheel? I reckon there's room for all three of us."

"Thanks, Grandpa. That would be great." But she couldn't help thinking, *I wish it was just me and Danny T.*

# The Wish

TWO DAYS LATER, Meghan picked up the postcard, half-buried in the mail on the kitchen counter. She instantly recognized the writing, with each M oversized and curving high, like the hills of a roller coaster:

*To Miss Meghan Michaela McCoy-Lee*

*Happy Birthday! I hope this is the best year ever!!*

*Hugs and kisses and lotsa love,*
*Mom*

*P.S. We're performing in Oregon this year—I'll come for a nice long visit.*

Sure you will.

Meghan flipped the postcard over. In big gold letters along the top of the card: *Ringman Brothers' Traveling Circus,* with a picture of her mother, Mimi the Magnificent, waiting to be shot out of a cannon. A clown leaned over to light the fuse.

Meghan opened the kitchen door and walked out to the garden, studying the postcard in the bright sunlight. Her mother seemed to be staring right at her, smiling from beneath her sequined headdress. A wide swath of green covered each eyelid. Usually her mom didn't wear much makeup. Or maybe she did, now.

Until six years ago, they'd both lived here in the old wooden house with Grandpa. On Sundays, after he left for church, they played Palace. They curtsied and bowed and said "Yes, M'lady," and "If you please." On those days Meghan got to wear her mother's orange spice perfume.

Meghan folded the postcard in half and slid it into her pocket. She flopped down on the grass and leaned back, gazing up at the sky. Butterflies swooped and dived in the warm summer air, their wings flashing gold in the afternoon light.

*Butterflies must be the happiest creatures on earth. They don't need a mother. All they need is their wings.*

She flipped onto her stomach and plucked a dandelion, staring at the ball of white fluff. *Make a wish . . .*

A pair of butterflies chased each other to and fro in a private game—happiness in motion. "I wish I could fly," Meghan said, her words soft but clear. She took a deep breath, puffed out her cheeks, and blew hard. The dandelion fluff floated away.

Meghan stood and brushed off her knees. Grandpa was working the weedy patch at the far end of the garden. "Grandpa! Want some help?"

He looked up and waved. "Grab a hoe!"

..

*Chop, chop, scrape.* Meghan tossed the weed clumps into a pile, tightened her grip on the handle, and began again. *Chop, chop, scrape*—she worked in rhythm, clearing one long row after another. Her arms ached from pounding the sun baked earth. She stopped for a minute. "What's going to replace the weeds?"

Grandpa paused and leaned on his hoe. "We'll plant a bit of grass seed and have a proper lawn next to the rose garden, like the president."

He took a few steps across the rocky soil. "I'll build us a table and chairs and put them here." He swung his hoe over his shoulder and gave the ground a hard whack. "Finally found the right spot for our fancy garden parties." He glanced at her and chuckled.

Meghan smiled. There was nothing fancy about his weather-worn house with its rambling garden and patchwork of fields, and Grandpa at a garden party with his old fishing hat, baggy overalls, and faded shirt…well, it just didn't fit.

He took a handkerchief from his pocket and wiped his forehead. "Take a break if you need to."

"I'm all right," she said, lifting her hoe and humming a little tune to the *chop, chop, scrape.*

Grandpa's ten acres ended at the edge of the thick forest. The house and garden looked out on his fields terraced below, and a narrow road sloped down from the house to the front gate. There were no other houses or farms in sight, only scrubby trees dotted the hills that descended into town. A crisscross of dirt roads connected the handful of dairy farms and organic growers like Grandpa. Apple Creek Middle School was barely visible beyond the last hill, with the soccer field half-hidden behind it.

"You're as strong as your dad was at your age," Grandpa said, glancing at the long, even rows of freshly tilled earth.

Meghan smiled and wiped her forehead on her sleeve. People told her she looked like her mom—same gold-flecked green eyes and honey colored hair—but she liked being compared to her dad. He'd been a hero.

Grandpa propped his hoe against the side of a wheelbarrow. "That's enough for now. My old bones need a rest, and we've both had enough sun today." He always wore a long-sleeved shirt for sun protection, but his face and hands were weathered to a dark tan. He settled onto the bench under the giant oak tree and patted the space beside him. "Come get some shade, darlin'."

Meghan sank onto the bench and leaned against him, watching the butterflies move from flower to flower. The shadows were lengthening, it was almost time for supper. She fished the card out of her pocket. "I got a postcard from Mom."

"I know. I didn't mean to read your mail, but with a postcard it's hard not to." He wrapped his arm around her shoulders.

A lump bloomed in Meghan's throat. She swallowed hard. "I thought maybe she'd call last week, on my actual birthday. Not that I'm surprised or anything."

Grandpa hugged her shoulders tighter. "One of these days she'll come home and explain why she's been gone so long."

"I bet I'm the only girl in the entire world whose mother ran off to join the circus. Who does that? It's ridiculous." Meghan tilted her head back and stared up at the gray-green leaves of the giant oak tree. "Sometimes it feels like she's dead, too."

Meghan closed her eyes and thought about her dad, David Walker Lee. She remembered how tall he was, and how good he smelled, a mixture of soap and freshly cut grass. And she remembered how he swung her high onto his shoulders when her feet got tired of walking.

She'd been sitting at the kitchen table drawing a picture when the fire chief knocked on the door. She heard him say, "I'm so sorry, Mimi," then quiet words. He'd tried to steer her mom into a chair, but she just crumpled to the floor.

After the chief left, her mom told her that Dad had run into a house to save a little girl. He lifted the girl out of her bedroom window and handed her to a fireman waiting below—and then the roof collapsed. Dad's badge and helmet were on permanent display in the big glass case at the fire station.

Meghan sighed and opened her eyes. An inchworm dropped in front of her face, dangling on a silk thread from the branch above. Grandpa gently pinched the line free and lowered the tiny creature into the grass. "Your mother tried hard," he said, sitting up again, "but she's not good at doing things kids need, like remembering to pack your lunch for school, or getting you to bed on time…she knew it would be better if you stayed here with me."

"But I was never hungry or anything." Meghan's voice was thick with unshed tears. "She was a *great* mother."

"She was a great mother when your dad was alive. The three of you were like a solar system, with you in the center and your mother and dad spinning around you. Only he was the gravity that held you all together. Without him she, uh…without him she—"

Meghan finished the sentence for him. "Without him she floated away. And never came back." She squeezed her eyes shut for a moment.

Grandpa gazed at her face, his eyes steady and kind. "Before your dad died, she played with you all the time, like she was a kid herself. Do you remember the beautiful dresses and costumes she made you, and that huge mural in your room? It covered the whole wall."

"There were clouds on the ceiling." Meghan wiped the corners of her eyes with the back of her hand. "And a pink and white castle with a moat, and a knight on a speckled horse. She never painted a princess. I was supposed to be the princess."

Grandpa nodded. "Your mother is a true artist."

"But why won't she come see me?" A wave of dread welled in her stomach. She had wondered for a long time. *Just say it.* "Does she have another family now?"

He waited until her eyes met his. "I'm certain she would tell me if I had another grandchild. No need to fret about that."

"Then *why*, Grandpa? It's been six years! Circuses travel all the time. She's probably been a few hours away from here and we didn't even know it."

The sun had sunk low in the sky, and leaves swished softly in the breeze. Grandpa stood and stretched. "Your mother is a complicated person, Meghan. Can't say I fully understand her myself. But she loves you very much, that's something I know for sure."

Meghan blinked hard, staring at the ground as if it held all the answers.

Grandpa reached out his hand. "Come on, let's get supper started."

Meghan grabbed his hand and pulled herself up from the bench.

CHAPTER THREE

# The Secret

THE NEXT MORNING was Sunday, sleep-in-late day, or sometimes church, if Grandpa was in the mood to go. But he would have woken her by now. Meghan padded into the kitchen and rummaged through the cupboards. She dropped two thick slices of bread into the toaster, then slathered the toast with butter before mixing sugar and cinnamon and sprinkling it on top. She took a bite. The sugar granules crunched sweet in her mouth, not yet melted into the butter. She poured a glass of milk, balanced the glass on the plate with her toast, and opened the door with her free hand.

The dew soaked her feet. Meghan sat sideways in one of the big wooden chairs and tucked her feet up off the grass. She munched on her toast and stared out over the hills, still grasping at images from the odd dream she'd had last night. For the first few years after her mom had left, she'd had nightmares about falling from a hot air balloon and dropping through the sky, waking night after night with her heart pounding and the back of her neck damp with sweat. Last night she had the dream again, but as she fell through the clouds a pair of golden-brown wings sprouted between her shoulder blades. She flew for hours, flapping hard to soar above snowy mountains, then swooping low over a meadow filled with wildflowers, the breeze pressing against her like a human kite. It was wonderful!

Grandpa broke into her thoughts, whistling in the distance. She liked the melody—he called it his morning music, a lively old Irish tune. He was resting on the bench under the giant oak tree at the far end of the garden. Meghan waved at him, then tossed the last crust of her cinnamon toast to a bluebird that pecked in the grass nearby.

She was too old to play pretend, but no one was watching, except Grandpa. Meghan stretched out her arms and ran full speed past the corn patch at the top of the garden, fluttered her arms as she skipped between the lettuce and tomatoes, then zigzagged through the green bean frames before circling wide around the roses, her arms held straight like she was gliding on air. With a final leap, she soared across a muddy patch and jogged over to Grandpa, plopping down hard on the bench next to him.

Grandpa chuckled. "That was an impressive flight. Thought you'd flatten the corn, rushing by so fast."

He closed his eyes. "You remind me of myself when I was a boy, running through the garden, pretending I could fly." He blinked his eyes open.

"Like me?"

He nodded. "I was a lot like you."

"Did you wish you could grow wings?" she asked. "Not make-believe wings. Real wings."

Grandpa leaned against the back of the bench. "Well, most children wish they could fly, but maybe not if they thought it all the way through. Kids like to fit in with their friends, especially coming up on teenage years." He winked at her. "Wings hanging off your shoulders would make you mighty different from your friends."

"So?" Meghan said. "Different isn't bad, it's just… different." She sighed. "I wish I could fly." She leaned forward to watch a caterpillar inch up the tree trunk.

Grandpa raised one eyebrow. "Are you sure? It might be fun for a while, but think about it, darlin'. Real wings would be a part of you—not a costume to peel off when you got tired of them."

Meghan shrugged. "I wouldn't want to take them off. I'd be happy, as long as I could fly. Last night I dreamed about flying—it felt so real." She told him how she sprouted wings and soared through the air.

"I had flying dreams myself," Grandpa said. He stared at her for a moment. "You'll keep having those dreams, now that you've started."

He sighed deeply. "You're more like a daughter to me than a granddaughter, Meghan, but it's your mother who should be explaining this to you." His voice dropped low. "It's about time I told you some things you ought to know." He cleared his throat and shifted uncomfortably on the bench, avoiding her eyes. "What I'm getting at is, uh…well, your dreams are perfectly natural for a young lady such as yourself."

*Oh no! Does he think flying has something to do with the birds and the bees?* Meghan blinked and glanced away.

"Come with me," Grandpa said. "I have something to show you." Meghan followed him up the garden path and into the kitchen.

*Please, not 'the talk'— this is NOT happening!* "Uh, Grandpa, remember when you signed that permission form so I could see a movie in science last year? Well, I already know about…"

Grandpa veered into the living room and pulled a book off the top shelf of the bookcase, before settling onto the couch. The book was old and black, the corners rounded with age, with *The McCoy Family Register* etched in faded gold letters, barely readable on the worn leather cover. Meghan sat next to him and breathed a quiet sigh of relief. Not a bird or bee in sight.

"This here's our family treasure—that's what my dad called it. Been passed down for generations." He stroked the cover gently, almost tenderly.

*Family treasure?* Her heart beat a little faster, but she knew she couldn't rush her grandpa.

"When I was twelve, same age as you, my parents showed me this book. It contains some unusual writings."

He pulled out his handkerchief and wiped the dust from the book's cover. "My dad called them 'magical writings'— magic words." Grandpa's eyes twinkled like he might be joking, but his voice sounded serious. "If you're sure about this flying business…"

Meghan nodded. *Magic words?*

Grandpa opened the book to a page marked with a green satin ribbon, the words written in elegant, old fashioned script:

> *"From shamrock hills of the Emerald Isle,*
> *Through ancient channels, I implore,*
> *Bestow with wings, born to this blood,*
> *A gift more rare than pots of gold.*
> *I call on you, 'tis birthright to ask,*
> *And set loose magic from days gone past.*
> *Grant this boon, no more to lack,*
> *Once I ask, no turning back."*

He finished reading and looked at her, waiting.

She leaned over and carefully read each line. "What is 'wings born to this blood' and 'birthright'?" Her heart began to pound. "It almost sounds like people in our family could fly. Is this supposed to be some kind of spell?"

"I don't know if it's rightly called a spell." He paused, searching for words. "But you're right about 'born to this blood.' My grandfather told me stories that were passed down from the olden days—he said our ancestors were born with wings."

Meghan's eyes widened. "No way! You're kidding, right?"

Grandpa's eyes crinkled into a smile. "It sounds pretty far-fetched, but who knows, maybe these ancient writings can wake up those old flying genes." He tapped the page. "Now, there's nothing in here about the timing, best to say it as much as you can, if you're serious about this. But you've got to be sure—there's no turning back once it's done."

"So, if I say the words and the timing is right, wings will magically grow on my back?" If that was true, he would have done it himself. "Come on, Grandpa, you know that's impossible."

He chuckled. "Improbable, but not impossible." He glanced over his shoulder at the window that looked over the garden. "But there's more to it. The words is your part, but you've got to have help from nature too, especially butterflies. It won't work without butterflies. Their wings seal the magic."

Meghan sighed. *Magic words? Butterflies?* Maybe he really believed some old story his grandfather told him, but that didn't make it real. She managed a half-hearted smile. "It's definitely a cool old book, and a cool old poem. Thanks for showing me."

"You can say the words, or not. Your choice." He smiled at her and gently closed the book.

Might as well go along—she had nothing to lose, even if it was completely impossible. Meghan reached for the book.

"Don't flip to any other pages."

She looked up. "Why, is there more 'magic?'"

"There's poems and songs, recipes. And maybe one or two other things." He winked at her. "But one thing at a time."

Meghan studied the words, reading each line again and again until she had memorized the poem or spell or whatever it was—then she closed the cover with a soft thump. A faint cloud of dust puffed up from the pages and hung in the air. For a moment, the dust shimmered with a greenish glow. Probably a reflection from the green satin bookmark.

"Thanks, Grandpa." Meghan handed the book back to him.

He nodded and got up from the couch to slide the book back into its spot on the top shelf of the bookcase. "Now don't go telling none of your friends about this. We can't have kids chasing our butterflies."

*Are you kidding? My friends would think I was a complete idiot.* But she couldn't resist at least trying. "Don't worry," she said. "I won't tell a soul. 'From shamrock hills of the Emerald Isle...'"

As Meghan recited the words she thought she heard Grandpa murmur, "Good Lord, what have we started?"

He cleared his throat and leaned backward to stretch. "Ready to give me a hand with the strawberries before it gets too hot?"

"Sure," Meghan said. "I'll catch a butterfly along the way."

Grandpa shook his head. "Their wings might break if you grab at them. Just come up real quiet and wait for one to land on you. That's how to do it."

••

Every morning they worked together in the fields. At lunchtime, Grandpa walked along the hard dirt road that curved up to his house, but Meghan cut straight across the hillside and climbed the fence at the far edge of the garden, treading softly and following the butterflies that zinged back and forth through the air. She stretched out her arms like a tree, but the butterflies wouldn't land on her.

After lunch, she snuck up on them as they flitted through the honeysuckle vines that curled around the front gate posts. She knelt and wove her hands through the leaves, but the butterflies weren't fooled. They landed on the flowers, not her fingers.

Days turned into weeks, and still no butterfly. Time for a new plan…maybe she could reach the butterflies that clustered on the sunflowers by the northeast fence, the line between the garden and the edge of the forest.

Meghan ran to the house, stopping in the kitchen to lift a chair off the ground, testing its weight. Too heavy. Her great-grandfather had made it himself out of dark walnut, strong enough to last for generations.

She set it down and searched the house: two upholstered chairs, an antique high-back with a wicker bottom, and a bulky leather office chair in Grandpa's room. A ladder would be too big…the kitchen chair would have to do. She picked it up and headed out to the garden.

It was a long way to the sunflowers. She passed the carrots and the Brussels sprouts, then the broccoli and summer squash. The muscles in her arms ached, and her right hand turned numb. It didn't help that her brain kept telling her this was stupid to be doing in the first place.

She put the chair down and rubbed her hands. The wood had pressed red lines into her palms. Another fifty feet to go.

Three butterflies perched on top of the tallest sun-flower. This was it. She climbed onto the chair and stood, very slowly.

The butterflies hadn't noticed her. She stretched out her hand and softly spoke the magic words:

> *"From shamrock hills of the Emerald Isle,*
> *Through ancient channels, I implore,*
> *Bestow with wings, born to this blood,*
> *A gift more rare than pots of gold.*
> *I call on you, 'tis birthright to ask,*
> *And set loose magic from days gone past.*
> *Grant this boon, no more to lack,*
> *Once I ask, no turning back."*

She held her hand an inch away from the nearest butterfly. It rested with its brown and gold speckled wings half-open, catching the warmth of the late day sun.

Meghan waited, hand steady, breathing in and out in calm, slow breaths. Minutes ticked by, but the butterfly remained motionless.

*Come on, I won't hurt you.* Her arm started shaking from holding it out so long.

Maybe if she touched the butterfly's leg ever so gently, it would step onto—

Oh no! The butterfly sensed her hand and darted away. The others scattered behind it. Meghan sighed. If she stood still and waited, they might come back.

A familiar sound drew closer. Grandpa's boots, clomping along the garden path.

# Butterfly Magic

"I WAS MAKING MYSELF a cup of tea," Grandpa said, "and something didn't seem quite right. One of the chairs had up and walked away." He chuckled. "But now I see you two are together. Mystery solved."

Meghan's cheeks turned warm. "I suppose you've been laughing the whole time, watching me chase after butterflies."

"Have I ever laughed at you?" Grandpa reached out his hand. "Come with me."

Meghan let him help her down from the chair. He led the way, weaving through the summer squash vines and onto the main path. At the far end of the garden, by the patch they'd cleared earlier that summer, he stopped and took off his work boots before stepping onto the tender shoots of new grass.

"I thought we weren't supposed to walk on the grass yet."

Grandpa raised a finger to his lips. "It's okay," he whispered, "just walk softly."

Meghan slipped off her shoes and picked her way across the grass. She sat down next to him and watched the butterflies that flitted above the roses. It was quiet— unnaturally quiet. No afternoon breeze rustled the leaves.

Grandpa leaned close and whispered, "You can't catch butterfly magic. It has to catch you."

Meghan no longer cared that none of this made sense. Grandpa believed it, and she wanted to believe it too. If she had wings she could go anywhere, maybe even find her mom. And flying would be amazing! But it was more than that now. For the past two weeks she'd had the flying dream almost every night—and woke feeling confused and sad to find her dream-wings had disappeared. In those hazy, half-awake minutes she felt incomplete, like she was missing her arms or legs.

The sun warmed her head and the rose bushes cast dappled shadows on the grass. The rich, sweet scent of rose blossoms filled the air. Only the trill of distant songbirds disturbed the warm stillness.

Time trickled by. Thirty minutes, one hour…

Meghan's head tilted forward and her eyelids grew heavy—

A butterfly fluttered around her face, then landed on her shoulder. Meghan snapped alert with a gasp. She sat motionless, barely breathing, watching the butterfly solemnly open and close its wings. She glanced sideways at Grandpa, careful not to move her head. He winked at her, eyes shining, but sat as still as a rock.

A fresh, strong breeze rustled the rose bushes. The butterfly pivoted and looked her full in the face, fluttered its wings, and soared away on the breeze.

"Goodbye!" Meghan called softly. She watched until the butterfly disappeared in the garden's deepening shadows.

Meghan stood and reached out her hand. "Thanks, Grandpa," she whispered.

"Don't thank me yet," he said, grasping her hand and pulling himself up. "Let's not count on anything, but it won't hurt to be hopeful."

••

AT BEDTIME, MEGHAN pulled the covers up to her chin.

"It's a full moon," Grandpa said.

She propped herself up on one elbow and gazed out the window. Stars pulsed against the blue-black sky, and the ancient moon glowed cool and bright. Meghan sighed, and rested her head back on her pillow. "Grandpa," she said, her voice already drowsy, "do you think the spell will work?"

"Let's say it together," he said, and sat down on the edge of her bed. Meghan closed her eyes.

*"From shamrock hills of the Emerald Isle,*
*Through ancient channels, I implore,*

*Bestow with wings, born to this blood,*
*A gift more rare than pots of gold.*
*I call on you, 'tis birthright to ask,*
*And set loose magic from days gone past…"*

The last thing she remembered was Grandpa tucking the blankets around her like a cocoon.

••

Sunlight streamed around the edges of the curtains—which were moving in the breeze. Grandpa must have opened the window last night before he left.

Meghan blinked her eyes closed. *It's Sunday, I can sleep in late.* She rolled onto her back.

What in the world was underneath her? She shoved her hand against—

*Ouch!* Whatever she was lying on was part of her!

A dream. She must be dreaming. *Maybe I'll fly over that meadow again.* She breathed quietly, willing her mind to go deeper into her dream.

*Tick, tick.* The clock in the hall wound into its double click before softly chiming the hour. She shifted onto her side, pinning the tip of her arm beneath her. The tip of her arm?

Her heart clanged in her chest, jolting her fully awake.

Meghan sprang out of bed and whipped her nightgown over her head. She turned and looked in the mirror above her dresser.

Two wings hung against her back, golden-brown and edged with a pattern of green dots and swirls.

*Okay, this feels real, but it's not. It can't be.* She pinched herself hard on the leg.

It hurt. And her shoulders hurt too, a deep ache that radiated across her upper back.

Her heartbeat gonged in her ears. *Dreams don't hurt. The spell must have worked!*

Her wings throbbed and prickled like limbs that had fallen asleep. She rotated them in a semicircle, flexing new muscles between her shoulder blades. Slowly the tingly pins and needles feeling disappeared.

She flapped them one at a time like the rudder of a sailboat, each wing gliding out from the hollow between her shoulder blades. Long bands of flexible cartilage allowed the wings to collapse in sections, folding together and opening like a fan. They looked like leathery bird wings, but with thin ribs running through, and upper and lower sections, like a butterfly. When she closed them, the two wings folded in on themselves and hung neatly against her back—hardly noticeable.

Meghan spread her wings wide and flapped as fast as she could.

*Ouch!* Her head bumped the ceiling.

She dropped with a thud. *Better try this outside... but not in just my undies.*

Her hands shook with excitement as she rummaged through her dresser drawers, looking for shorts and a tank top with narrow straps. Perfect—a faded old one of her mom's, nice and stretchy. Meghan had worn it as a nightgown when she was little. She pulled the shirt over her head and eased her wings through the back, one at a time. They were flexible and light, but strong.

Meghan crossed the room and climbed onto the windowsill, dangling her legs outside. She took a deep breath and leaned forward, flapping hard. Her wings caught the air like a sail full of wind. She was higher than the house!

*This is incredible!* Meghan arched her back and straightened her legs, flapped faster, shot over the treetops, and then twirled in wide loops before landing on the grass.

"Grandpa! Look at me!" She flapped her wings and took off again.

Grandpa opened the kitchen door and stepped outside. "Where are you?"

"Up here!" she called, smiling down from the sky.

"You did it!"

"Thanks to you!" Her voice rang with joy.

He grinned as she fluttered and twirled closer to the ground. "I only told you the words. The rest was up to you, and the butterflies."

Meghan shot up again, flying a figure eight high above his head.

"Come here for a minute," Grandpa called, motioning with his hand. "I want to show you something."

Meghan glided toward him. She landed hard, bending her knees but managing to stay upright. She laughed. "Landing's going to take a little practice!"

Grandpa chuckled softly. "Yes, landing does take a bit of practice." He smiled at her and then turned around, shrugging off his long-sleeved shirt.

Meghan gasped—hanging through two slits in his under- shirt was a pair of shiny wings, each one folded flat against his back. "They're just like mine! But why didn't you tell me?"

"I've wanted to for a long time. It needed to be a secret, at least until you were old enough." With a quick flick, he opened his wings. "Now, let's see how fast you can fly. Tag! I'm It!"

Meghan laughed and flapped into the air.

"Gotcha!" Grandpa said, tagging her foot. Meghan twirled and raced after him. He swooped low over the corn and green beans before zooming past the top of the giant oak tree.

Meghan was right behind him.

"Tag!" she said, her fingers skimming the back of his ankle. "You're It!" They flew faster and faster. The thump, thump, thump of their wings sounded like the wind softly clapping.

Meghan turned to look at Apple Creek Middle School, way down at the bottom of the last hill. She wished the kids from school could see her, but even if she flew closer, summer session was already over. Only a few cows dotted the hills, grazing. *I can't wait to show Jade … and Danny.*

Grandpa hovered in the air, his wings flapping forward and then backward, keeping him in one place. "Let's take a rest," he said. "My old wings can't keep up with yours."

Meghan laughed. "You're not old."

"Too old to keep up with you!" He grinned. "I just need to catch my breath."

As soon as they landed on the grass, he examined Meghan's wings. "No regrets, I hope? You're happy?"

"Are you kidding? Today is the happiest day of my life!"

Grandpa nodded. "It's a marvelous thing indeed. Not many folks get a gift like this—only us McCoys, far as I know." His smile faded. "And that's what I got to warn you about. We took a chance today, flying out in the open like this." He gazed over the crest of the hill. "Can't think of the last time someone came around without calling, but it's not worth the risk. Only other McCoys can know about our wings, not that there's many of us left."

"Other McCoys? So, my mom grew wings too, when she was my age?"

Grandpa drew a sharp breath. "Your mother was interested in clothes, and boys—and talking on the phone. Lord knows that girl liked to talk on the phone. When it came to wings, your mother, well, she ..." He frowned and folded his wings tight against his back. "Like I was saying, this has to stay secret."

"But Grandpa! I want to show my friends. I won't tell them about our family book or the butterflies, but they have to see me fly!"

"It's more complicated than that, darlin'." Grandpa took a handkerchief from his pocket and dabbed the perspiration off his forehead. "I can tell you're bursting with excitement, and you should be—but one person talks to another, and before long we've got a big problem."

He wrapped his arm around her shoulders, gently steering her down the path toward the bench by the old oak tree. "Let me tell you about another McCoy who had wings. He wasn't much older than you…"

# CHAPTER FIVE

# The Sideshow

"LONG BEFORE I was born," Grandpa said, brushing oak leaves off the bench, "every McCoy baby came into the world with wings. Couldn't use them until they hardened up—around three or four years old, depending—but boy or girl, they were all born with wings on their backs. It's in our genes. And lucky for you they're strong genes," he added, glancing at her wings. "I wasn't sure they'd hold up after so many generations."

They settled onto the bench. Meghan turned toward him, listening intently.

"Back in 1896, when my great-grandparents' son Emmet was fourteen, a traveling sideshow came to Carrick—that's the little town in Ireland where they lived. There was a man who ate nails, a snake charmer, a bearded lady…well, when the sideshow left town three days later, Emmet was gone."

"What happened? Did they steal him?"

"He left a note, said he was seeking his fortune and all that rot. Just about broke his family's heart, especially his mother's. They were very close."

Meghan tried to imagine leaving her mother, if her mother hadn't left her first. "Didn't they try to find him?"

"They went to the police—but you got to remember, there was no internet and not many phones in those days." Grandpa sighed. "If a kid up and ran away, he was pretty much gone. No one knew where the sideshow was traveling next, and his parents couldn't wander off looking for him. They had a farm to tend, and two other children to raise."

He pressed his lips together, thinking. "Let's see, Emmet's mother and father would be your…" He counted the generations on his fingers. "Great, great, great, grand-parents. Luke and Meara McCoy.

Eight years later they went to visit an old school friend of Meara's, lived in a town near the River Shannon. The good Lord put Luke and Meara in the right place at the right time—just so happened the sideshow was traveling through there." The lines in his forehead furrowed deeper. "That night they went to the show…"

"What, Grandpa? Did they find him?"

"Oh, they found him, all right. He was bruised and sickly, bone thin, a prisoner of those evil people."

"You mean the sideshow people kidnapped him?"

"He joined of his own free will, but when he started missing his family and wanted to go home, it turned out he was too valuable. They wouldn't let him leave. He flew around inside a tent for the crowds, but they kept his wings strapped down when he wasn't performing."

"That's terrible! Couldn't he sneak away?"

Grandpa shook his head. "One night he tried, almost got out of his straps while everyone was sleeping. The owner's sons caught him, beat poor Emmet until he was near dead. From that night on, they made him sleep in a cage like an animal, kept him almost starved to break his spirit so he wouldn't try it again."

Meghan leaned forward on the bench. "But they let him go after his parents found him, right?"

"Yes, darlin', they let him go. They had no choice. His parents went to the police—they set Emmet free, and then arrested that horrible man and his sons. After that the McCoy clan split apart. Some moved clear across Ireland to a town called Killarney, others settled in England, and a few came to America."

"That must be our branch of the family."

Grandpa nodded. "Luke and Meara settled in Killarney with Emmet. His sister Lara married a preacher's son and had four children, lived near her folks. But the oldest son, Marcus, well, he struck out for America. He bought this land in 1905. Plenty of space to grow crops—and fly without being spotted, at least back in the days when there weren't so many people living in these parts. This was his farm."

Grandpa sighed. "Aunts, uncles, old folks and young, they all scattered like seeds in the wind. Vanished from sight, left friends behind without a word of goodbye."

"I don't get it," Meghan said. "If the sideshow people were in jail, why did the McCoys move away?"

Grandpa paused and wiped the back of his neck with his handkerchief. "They learned a lesson that didn't need repeating," he said, and tucked the handkerchief back in his pocket. "There are plenty of people in this world like the folks from the sideshow, darlin'. They'll try to take advantage of you, make money off you. My great-grandparents knew sooner or later someone else would find a way to steal another McCoy child." He shook his head. "From that day on, the McCoys never showed their wings again."

Meghan sat quietly, imagining her relatives moving in secret, leaving all their friends behind. "What happened to Emmet?" she asked.

Grandpa stared out at the patchwork of fields beneath the hill. "I wish the story had a happy ending," he said, "but Emmet was a shadow of the man he could have been. Beaten, starved, living in a cage for eight years—he never did get over it. Never married, lived a quiet life with his parents. Emmet died before they did, caught pneumonia when he was twenty-nine."

Meghan swallowed past the lump in her throat. She almost felt like she knew him. "But that couldn't happen nowadays, could it? My picture would be all over the place if I got stolen. It's not like the olden days."

Grandpa nodded. "I'm not so worried about you getting stolen, what with the internet and cell phones everywhere." His eyebrows knitted together. "But you show the world your wings and the newspapers, TV reporters, scientists—they'd swarm on us like ants on sugar. We'd be prisoners in our own home."

"But only for a little while, don't you think?" Meghan twisted her long hair into a loose knot and leaned against the back of the bench. "What could they really do, if you think about it. They'd take our picture and ask a bunch of questions. It could be a scientific mystery, like being born with a tail. After all, we have wings in our family—no one needs to know about the magic part. Before you know it, another event would hit the news and everyone would move on. You see it happen that way all the time. It wouldn't be that big a deal if reporters wanted to take my picture. I wouldn't mind too much."

"You might not—but I would." Grandpa swept his hand out, gesturing toward the rolling hills and the thick forest behind his property. "You see any neighbors? If I want to see folks I go into town."

"Well how about if it's only me?" Meghan asked. "You wouldn't have to show *your* wings, if you don't want to." She watched a spotted falcon soaring over the lower field. "Flying is wonderful—I want to do it all the time! It almost seems like you're ashamed of your wings, Grandpa. So, don't fly. But don't keep me from it!"

Grandpa took in a sharp breath. "I'm not ashamed, darlin', that's not the word." He paused and gazed out at the highway, a thin, hazy line in the distance. "We've been hiding for years, generation after generation. I just kept on hiding."

He turned and looked at Meghan. "Maybe now it's time to stop. This is America, people have rights. And I never expected you to give up flying! For McCoys, flying is an itch that's got to get scratched."

He winked at her. "I've been flying at sunup most mornings since I was your age." He gestured toward the forest that curved around the back of his property. "If you don't mind losing a little sleep, I'll take you with me."

"Thanks, Grandpa. That'll be great! But I still want to show my friends. And I want to fly around, like to school or the library, or to Jade's house." She gazed up at him. "Wings are a part of me now. I don't want to hide them."

He nodded. "I understand, darlin', but I need time to think this all the way through and come up with a plan. So for now, I'm trusting you to keep your flying to early morning-time, with me."

He locked eyes with her. "Slow down a wee bit, okay?"

# CHAPTER SIX

# Teen Trouble

MEGHAN SAT ON a thick branch of the apple tree by the front gate and gazed down the dirt road that wound its dusty way into town. Her school looked tiny from this distance, Apple Creek Middle School, a rectangle of gray in the distance. Back to school tomorrow—seventh grade.

She could hardly wait to see Jade. Neither one of them had a cell phone, otherwise Meghan would have called to tell Jade about her wings. Jade had spent the last three weeks at her cousin's house in Portland, her uncle was driving her home tonight—but tomorrow would be here soon, and she was definitely showing her wings to Jade, no matter what Grandpa said. Jade would never tell anybody.

A bee buzzed around Meghan's face. She shooed it away and shifted to a more comfortable position on the branch. So much had happened over the summer—seeing Greta at the fair, and Danny, and of course, her wings. *I wonder what Danny will think about my wings?*

Three teenagers on horseback clip-clopped around the bend. *I can't believe I didn't hear them!* They were talking and laughing, two girls riding side by side, and a boy in a cowboy hat trailing a few paces behind them.

Meghan's heart pounded. She reached back and tucked each bottom wing section underneath the top, like bending an arm at the elbow. Now her wings were folded to half their size. She leaned further into the tree, pressing against the thick trunk.

The riders were almost beneath her now. She glanced down at her shirt, a green tank top. It was good camouflage. Maybe they wouldn't see her.

One of the girls was Lena, a sixteen-year-old with dark blond hair pulled back in a ponytail. She was the youngest daughter of their only neighbor, a dairy farmer who lived a mile away. Their house and farm nestled in a small valley between the hills, hidden from view.

"Hi Meghan!" Lena called. "Can you give us some apples for our horses?"

Meghan waved and said, "I'll toss some down." *Why didn't I bring a shirt to cover my wings?* She reached for an apple but couldn't quite grab it. Three dangled above her head, slightly out of reach. It was an easy climb to the next branch, but she'd have to turn around—her wings would be facing the teens.

Meghan waited, hoping they'd look away for a moment.

They didn't.

She stared wide-eyed at an imaginary spot behind them, and then faked a small gasp of surprise. *Come on people, turn around. Don't you want to know what I'm looking at? It's absolutely fascinating!*

But the three riders kept peering up into the branches, waiting for Meghan to pick the apples and drop them for their horses. *Please, please look away…*

Lena's friend turned her head and said something Meghan couldn't hear. Lena nodded. "Are you stuck?" she called. "I'll climb up and help you." She handed her reins to her friend, preparing to dismount.

"No! Don't come up here!" Meghan's voice squeaked on its way out.

"Are you all right?" Lena asked.

Meghan didn't answer. *Maybe I should say I have a stomach ache and can't move. Don't get too close, I don't want anyone else to get sick.*

Her heart thundered in her chest. *No. I'm not going to lie…maybe it's meant to be.*

"I'm fine," she called down.

*Well, here goes.* She climbed onto the higher branch and began picking apples.

"Hey, what's that on her back?" Lena's friend flipped up her sunglasses.

*Sorry, Grandpa.* Meghan unfurled her wings and flew down from the tree.

"Whoa—are those real?" asked the boy with the cowboy hat.

"Oh, they're definitely real," Meghan said. She flew a loop around the top of the apple tree, hovered for a moment, and then fluttered to the ground.

"That is so cool! I've never heard of a person with wings."

Meghan smiled and shrugged her shoulders. "I woke up one morning a few weeks ago and found out that I grew wings. It's like when a person is born with a tail, sort of an extension of their tail bone. Only my wings happened when I was older." Her voice dropped low before trailing off. "I wasn't actually born with them …" She swallowed, making a soft gulping sound. Her explanation didn't quite sound believable.

"Yeah, but those aren't an extension of your shoulder blades," the boy said. "Those are full-on wings." He leaned back in his saddle and stared at Meghan. "We won't tell anyone if you're from another planet. We mean you no harm."

"I'm not an alien!" Meghan choked out a laugh. "I'm the same as everyone else, but suddenly I grew wings. Just lucky, I guess."

No one spoke.

Meghan kicked the ground. *Maybe this wasn't such a great idea.*

Lena shook her head. "Very funny, Meghan. You really had us going."

Lena's friend did not look convinced. She sat up in the saddle, boots poised to urge her horse away, far and fast.

Lena glanced over at her friend. "Don't freak—I've known her since she was little. Meghan is a normal kid, goes to A.C.M.S." She gestured down the hill toward Apple Creek Middle School, as if that explained everything.

"Where did you get them?" Lena asked. "I wore wings for Halloween about ten years ago, but they weren't a kind that actually worked." She smiled at Meghan. "How do they attach?"

Meghan's heart drummed a sickening beat. *Just stay calm, reassure them.* She walked up to Lena's horse and patted its side, holding out an apple. The horse snuffled it off her palm. "They attach between my shoulders, through my skin. They're a part of me, for real. But I'm not an alien or anything."

The teens glanced at each other, and then stared at Meghan as she fed apples to the other two horses.

The boy in the cowboy hat pulled out his phone. "Fly again so I can take a picture."

"I-I...I'm not sure if I should let anyone—"

"Meghan!" Grandpa yelled from the front door. "Please come inside! Immediately."

"Can you fly above the tree, like you did before? I just want to—"

"Sorry." Meghan folded her wings tight and reached around to tuck the bottom sections underneath their tops. She slowly backed away from Lena and the other two teens, her wings now bent to half their size, concealed behind her back. "I have to go in now."

Meghan's stomach lurched in waves of dread. Why hadn't she *climbed* down from the tree?

The teens stared at Meghan as she walked backward, her wings facing away from them, all the way up the steep slope that led to her front porch, and to Grandpa.

He closed the door behind her, locked it, then turned without speaking and headed for the kitchen. Meghan followed him.

"What in the world were you thinking?" Grandpa pulled out a chair and sat down. His breath came out in angry huffs. "We talked about this."

"I couldn't help it," Meghan said, her voice shaking a little. "I was in the apple tree and I didn't see them in time to get away and they wanted me to pick some apples for their horses—what was I supposed to do, lie to Lena? Tell her I was sick and couldn't move? Or tell her they were fake wings or something?"

Grandpa's eyes flashed. "I would never ask you to lie— but I never thought you'd be so careless, either. You could have worn an extra shirt, or carried one with you."

Meghan slumped into the chair across from him. "I know. I'm sorry, Grandpa." She swallowed a few times, gathering her thoughts. "I honestly didn't mean to, but I'm actually kind of glad it happened. I don't want to keep my wings covered forever. Really, I can handle it."

"You've rushed us into this when I directly asked you to wait." He turned toward the front window. "We don't need a mob of reporters asking questions—leastways, not before I figure out what to tell them."

"I told you, I won't say anything about our family book, or the butterflies. Ever." Meghan stared at her hands, picking at a hangnail until is hurt.

Grandpa nodded. "There wouldn't be a butterfly left for miles around." He sighed. "Wait here. I've got something I've been meaning to show you."

Meghan heard the closet door squeak in his bedroom down the hall, then thumps and rustling sounds. Something clattered to the ground.

A few minutes later he emerged carrying what looked like an old photo album. "This has been hidden for years, figured it was safe behind my fishing gear. Dumped the whole blasted box trying to get to it."

He set the album on the kitchen counter and opened to the first page. "This here's Meara McCoy, your great-great-great-grandmother, Emmet's mother—and there's her wings."

# CHAPTER SEVEN

# The Face in the Meara

MEGHAN LEANED OVER the album and studied the photo. It was old, its edges curled with age. Meara's eyes stared back at her, full of smarts and spirit.

"She was so pretty, Grandpa. How old was she when this was taken?"

"Not much older than you. This is from her eighth-grade graduation. She was lucky—in those days most children didn't get past the sixth grade." He hunched over the faded photograph. "Look at those eyes. You two could be sisters."

He turned the page to show Meara as a young woman standing with his great-grandfather, both turned slightly away from the camera, dressed in old-fashioned wedding clothes. Meara's wings hung through slits in the back of her simple white gown.

"There's more." He flipped through the pages, pointing out aunts and uncles and many-times great relatives, most of them with wings.

"This is incredible!" Meghan examined each face like she was memorizing it.

Grandpa smiled down on the long gone McCoys. "No one had the heart to destroy the album after the clan began hiding their wings." He turned to a page in the middle. "Here's a picture of Luke and Meara with their children. Emmet looks to be about three years old. That's his brother Marcus and his sister Lara." The tips of their wings peeked out from behind their backs.

Meghan studied Emmet's small, oval face. A fringe of soft brown hair swept across his forehead, and a tiny smile curled the edges of his mouth. He sat on his mother's lap with his brother and sister standing next to him, their faces solemn. *Oh Emmet, I wish I could warn you.*

"My father gave me the album before he died," Grandpa said. "I was planning to show you when you were old enough to keep a secret."

Meghan's face grew warm. "I'm really sorry, Grandpa."

"If you hadn't grown wings, there wouldn't be a reason to show you these pictures—I would have waited a few years. That's all I meant. I wasn't trying to beat you down for making a mistake with Lena and those other kids." He opened his arms wide. "I forgive you, okay? Now come give me a hug."

Meghan's eyes welled. She blinked hard.

"No need for tears, darlin'." He wrapped his arms around her and kissed the top of her head before gently pushing away. "We'll deal with whatever comes." He pointed to the window. "And we better see if anyone's coming our way."

Meghan stood at the edge of the large kitchen window, her eyes scanning the steep driveway and long stretch of road outside the front gate. The horseback riders must have called their friends—now there were seven teenagers. She moved to the living room and tightened the wooden slats of the shades, in case one of the teens tried to creep along the side of the house. There were still some gaps, but it would have to do.

The floorboards creaked behind her. Grandpa, with the photo album held close to his chest. "I checked our bedroom windows. All clear."

"All clear here, too," Meghan said. "The gate is still closed. They're all standing around down at the road."

"I'll put this away," Grandpa said, "but you can look at it whenever you like." He made a space for the album on the top shelf of the bookcase, and then pulled out *The McCoy Family Register*. "You finally got to meet the rest of the family. There have been generations of McCoys with wings, and now you." His eyes crinkled into a smile. "You're a 'real McCoy.'"

Meghan managed a small laugh, and the tightness in her stomach eased. He really had forgiven her.

He settled onto the couch. "In Ireland," he said, patting the space next to him, "folks grew up knowing about leprechauns and fairies and all sorts of magical goings-on. Wings was a big deal, but not unheard of." The lines in his forehead deepened. "Here in America it's a whole different story."

Meghan moved away from the window and sat next to him on the couch. "Are there real leprechauns and fairies?" she asked. "I thought that was only a legend."

"Well, legends have to start somewhere. Most have a seed of truth in them."

"So, we're actually related to fairies?"

He laughed. "It's a strong possibility, wouldn't you say?" He wiggled his wings up and down. "One thing's certain: there's magic in the sap of our family tree—we've got wings to prove it."

Grandpa's face turned serious. "My understanding is our ancestors were part fairy-folk," he said, "but not the wee little ones with fancy colored wings—our people weren't that tiny." He leaned against the back of the couch. "Butterflies are related to fairy-folk, like distant cousins, at least that's how my grandfather explained it. Somehow, it's all connected—butterflies, fairies, and our family, the real McCoys." He chuckled, enjoying his joke again. "We'll never know all the answers, only what's in the family book."

Meghan touched the worn cover. "Who wrote this, Grandpa? I can tell it's very old."

He opened to the title page. There was nothing written there, only a faded green shamrock stamped in the center of the yellowed paper. "It's a family journal, belongs to all of us. The entries were written over many generations, some dating back hundreds of years. Most of them aren't signed, but I recognize my grandmother's handwriting for one of the blessings. She had beautiful penmanship."

He smiled at Meghan. "I was very close to my grandparents. We all lived here together when I was a boy, three generations in the same house. Just like you and your mom when you two moved in." He winked at her. "But I think you're asking about the magic bits, not your great-grandmother's penmanship."

Meghan leaned closer, listening intently.

"Many generations ago, someone wrote down those flying words—my guess is it was the very same person who had wings and married into the family. Whoever it was, they must have understood that the genes for flying would get diluted with each passing generation, and over time McCoy babies would not be born with wings."

His eyes crinkled as he held back a grin. "If we didn't have the magic words and the butterflies to give our old genes a boost, you and I would not be flyers." He twitched his wings underneath his shirt. Meghan smiled.

"My grandfather Marcus had two children, Lucia and Lakan, born right here on this farm. They were the last McCoys born with wings. Now, you know Lakan McCoy was my father. But can you imagine the two of them when they were little bitty children, flying around here in the garden?" He chuckled softly.

"There's Emmet." He tapped the branch where three lines held Emmet and his brother and sister's names. The branches thinned near the bottom. "Not too many of us left." He pointed to Meghan's name, written in his own distinctive cursive, perched beneath her parents.

"Is this another spell?" Meghan asked, turning the page and leaning closer to read a block of cramped script.

Grandpa closed the book with a soft thud. "We'll read more from time to time, but I'd rather you didn't look through the family register without my knowing about it. Can I trust you on that?"

Meghan nodded. That would be a hard promise to keep! What other spells were in the book?

Grandpa stood and slid the old book back into its place on the shelf. "When my grandfather Marcus first came to America," he said, settling onto the couch again, "he sprinkled earth from Ireland all around this property. Been talk about that for years, but only our family knows it's true."

He glanced at Meghan, his eyebrows pulling together in a deep frown. "We can't have reporters and scientists trampling our fields, digging up soil samples. They'll sneak into the garden and tear apart the roses looking for enchanted nectar—and who knows what they'll do to the butterflies. When you tell people about the flying McCoys, there are two words that never need to get brought up—butterflies, and magic."

"You can trust me, Grandpa. Don't you believe me?"

"I'm sorry, darlin'. I just don't think you realize what we're up against here." His voice dropped low. "If anyone finds out there's magic in our bloodline, it's not only the butterflies who'd be in danger. Scientists, even our own government—they'd want to do experiments on us. We've got to stick to the story about our family genes. It's the truth, you know I'd never ask you to lie—but telling more than that would be plain foolish. We'd be asking for trouble."

Meghan nodded. She would never tell anyone, not even Jade.

Grandpa walked into the kitchen, staying out of sight by ducking low and circling around to the side of the window. "They're coming in thick."

Meghan slipped in next to him and peered through the sliver of glass between the edge of the open curtain and the window frame. A group of teenagers had gathered at the gate. Meghan counted fifteen of them before Grandpa rolled the window shade down.

He took a box of tea out of the cupboard and began filling the kettle. "Chamomile? Or would you rather have mint?"

Meghan flicked on the overhead light. "Can we have both? I never tried it that way. Chamomile mint."

The phone rang. Grandpa picked it up. "Mike McCoy, here…What? My family is none of your concern. I'll thank you to mind your own business."

The phone rang again almost as soon as he put it down. "Hello? Now you listen here, my granddaughter is getting ready for school in the morning. We don't have time for this." He hung up. "Busybodies."

Meghan peeked out. Three teens on mountain bikes had joined the crowd, and a motorcycle was pulling up behind the haphazard line of cars already parked along one side of the road. The phone rang again.

"Channel Nine News?" Meghan froze until she caught the sly expression on Grandpa's face. "Wings? Now, who did you say reported this?" He paused, listening. "Ah, teenagers! What will they think of next, unicorns in my cornfield?"

Two other stations called, one right after the other. "Teenagers." Grandpa grinned into the phone. "They're getting my goose, those rascals." He chuckled good naturedly. "No, they didn't mean any harm by it. Just teenagers, up to their usual shenanigans." He laughed. "I might have pulled a prank or two myself, back in my day." After that, he unplugged the phone.

Meghan smiled, but gave him a long look. "That was kind of a lie, Grandpa."

He pressed his hands over his heart, like she had wounded him. "I didn't tell them one thing that wasn't true." He winked at her. "That, my darlin' is called 'misdirection,' a little fancy footwork to get them off our scent, at least for now."

The kettle began to whistle. He dropped two tea bags into a ceramic teapot and poured the steaming water over them. "Word will get out that it's a prank. It may hold them off, stop any reporters from poking around and asking questions. Let's hope so."

"When can I show people?" Meghan asked. "I don't want to keep my wings covered forever. It won't be like Emmet. I promise. I'll be careful."

Grandpa lifted the edge of the curtain and glanced out, and then turned back to look at her. "I know you'll be careful. Just give me time to come up with a plan."

••

THAT EVENING THEY cut wing-slits in Meghan's school shirts. "This will have to do for now," Grandpa said, snipping a few loose threads. "Your mother is bound to show up any day. She can dust off your grandma's old sewing machine and hem these edges."

"My mom? She's coming here? When is she coming?"

Grandpa shrugged. "Soon, I hope. I left a message for her at Ringman Brothers' headquarters."

The next time Meghan peeked out, more teens had flooded in. They all seemed to have a phone in their hands, calling or texting their friends.

By bedtime the news had spread all over town.

# Mean Greta

A GROUP OF STUDENTS stood talking at the edge of the school yard, their breath forming foggy clouds in the early morning chill.

"Looks like we fooled them reporters," Grandpa said. "When they weren't at our gate this morning, I thought they might be here." Students milled around the front sidewalk, a few headed toward the main office with their parents.

Meghan cringed inside her sweater. It was cream colored and came almost to her knees, with oversized buttons up the front and a matching self-tie belt…must have been in style a few decades ago, when her mom wore it. Grandpa had found it in the back of the hall closet. Meghan hated it, but the sweater was long enough to avoid getting cramps from folding her wings all day, and the thick cable knit completely concealed them, even when she took off her backpack.

Her stomach churned. She looked around. *Where's Jade?*

The bell rang. "It's going to be fine," Grandpa said. He gave her a hug. Meghan held on for a few extra seconds.

••

The entrance was thick with students jostling one another, pressing forward to their homerooms. A familiar voice called out. Meghan hesitated for a moment but kept going.

"Don't act like you didn't hear me," Greta said, breaking away from a cluster of girls standing together on the side of the hallway.

"Oh. Hi Greta." Meghan inched toward her homeroom. Hopefully Jade would already be there.

Greta flipped her glossy red hair behind her ear. "Someone told me you have *wings*?" Four girls flanked Greta, two on each side. They all moved together to block Meghan's way.

Greta stared at Meghan and slowly unscrewed the top of a tiny pot of lip gloss. "Well, we don't have all day." She dipped her pinky in the lip gloss, and then circled her already shiny lips.

Other students stopped or slowed down to see what was happening. Meghan took a step backward. "Uh, the second bell's going to ring soon. We'd better get to homeroom."

Greta smirked. "Don't worry, we have time." She scanned the faces of the crowd that had begun to gather. "I heard they're brown and shiny—like insect wings. Talk about freaky!" Some of the girls giggled.

"I would love to have wings," said a soft voice with an English accent. It belonged to Kayla, a slender girl with long dark hair and cinnamon skin whose family had moved from London last year. She had been assigned to Meghan's homeroom. Meghan didn't know her very well, but her heart surged with gratitude.

Greta stepped forward, close enough for Meghan to see the hard gleam in her eyes. "They've got to be fake. Still playing dress-up, I guess." She reached for the belt on Meghan's sweater.

Meghan backed away, her heartbeat clanging in her ears. "Stop it, Greta. We're going to be late."

"Excuse me, coming through!" Jade elbowed her way to Meghan, who had never been so glad to see anybody in her life. Jade glared at Greta and said, "Ever heard of personal space?"

"Oh, I'm *so* sorry." Greta stared wide-eyed at Meghan, blinking at her with exaggerated innocence. "I was only trying to help you take off that *interesting* sweater—it seems a little too warm for inside, but my mistake. I certainly didn't mean to upset you or your trendy little buddy." She blinked at Jade, stroking the sleeve of her own new sweater, made of soft merino wool in a beautiful shade of cranberry.

Meghan's face reddened like she'd been slapped. She knew Jade felt the sting too—she was wearing faded no-name jeans, scuffed boots, and a dark denim jacket she had almost outgrown. Meghan had never seen the shirt, but she could tell it wasn't new, probably a hand-me-down from her cousin.

Jade looped her arm through Meghan's. "Let's go," she said. "We'll walk in together."

"Whatever," Greta said, glancing around at her friends. "I guess she wants to show us later." Her eyes narrowed as her gaze rested on Meghan. "We can wait."

Kayla glided through the throng of students like a ballerina weaving across the stage. She moved to Meghan's other side and glared at Greta and her girls.

Meghan let out a breath she didn't realize she'd been holding. "Thanks," she said, her voice squeaking on its way out.

The three girls made their way to homeroom and slid into seats in the back row. Meghan's heartbeat settled to a slow thump. She took a deep breath, picked up the stack of back to school papers on her desk, and began filling in the blanks.

Jade leaned in close. "So…wings? What's up with that? Are you trying to mess with Greta's head?"

Meghan whispered, "We need to talk in private."

Jade nodded and went back to work on her papers.

A few minutes later, their teacher called out, "Everyone, please take the emergency information form home for your parents to sign. And turn in the yellow sheet before you leave," she added, raising her voice above the sound of the bell.

"Follow me," Meghan whispered, as they added their sheets of paper to the pile on the teacher's desk. They shuffled out the door with the other students.

Meghan veered toward the girls' locker room. "Do you mind being late for first period?"

"We can say we got confused about where we're supposed to be." Jade flashed a conspiratorial grin. "Quick, before anyone sees us."

The locker room was empty—P.E. electives didn't start until third period.

"Hold the door," Meghan said. Jade leaned against it just as someone pushed from the other side.

"Let me in. It's me."

"Me who?" Jade asked.

"Me Kayla." Jade opened the door enough for Kayla to squeeze in.

"Um, Kayla," Jade said. "This is kind of private."

"Oh." Her face flushed. "Sorry." She turned to leave.

Meghan shrugged, raising her eyebrows at Jade in an unspoken question.

"It's okay," Jade said, turning to Kayla. "You can stay. But help me hold the door."

Meghan took a deep breath and gazed back and forth between Jade and Kayla. "Okay, but you have to promise not to tell anyone."

Jade and Kayla nodded. "Our lips are sealed," Jade said.

"I-I guess…" Meghan glanced around the locker room. "So, I guess I'm just going to go ahead and do it." She slipped off her mother's old sweater and laid it on the bench.

"Ta-da!" She twirled around and snapped her wings open in one fluid movement.

Kayla's mouth dropped open.

Jade gasped. "You *do* have wings! Oh my gosh, Meghan, you're so lucky! I didn't believe the rumors—but why didn't you tell me before?" Her face clouded in a quick frown.

"You were at your cousin's," Meghan said, "and my grandfather was home last night. I couldn't just pick up the phone and blurt, 'Hey, guess what happened while you were in Portland? I grew wings. See you at school.' It would have taken too long to explain, and anyway, he wants me to keep it a secret until he figures out a plan—he's worried that scientists might try to do experiments on me."

Meghan told them about the winged relatives in her family, and how a few weeks ago she'd gone to sleep a normal girl, and woke to find she'd grown a pair of wings.

Kayla slowly shook her head, her eyes wide. "This is absolutely incredible! But no worries, your secret is safe with me." She raised her fingers to her lips and twisted an imaginary key. "I can't stand gossips and tattlers."

"Same here," Jade said, nodding at Kayla. She turned to Meghan. "Show us how they fly."

Meghan flapped upward and touched the ceiling with her fingertips, hovered in place for a few seconds, and then let her wings fold against her back as she landed.

Jade stared at her, speechless for a few moments. "That is so cool—I can hardly believe it! Can I touch one?"

"If you want to."

Jade left her place by the door and gently brushed her finger along the edge of one wing. "Wow, it's so smooth, but tough too—like leather. Do they feel heavy?"

Meghan shook her head. "They're actually pretty light. My backpack is a lot heavier."

"They're very flexible, wonderful how they collapse. Like bat wings." Kayla's English accent and the astonishment in her voice made it sound like she was narrating a documentary about a strange new species.

Meghan picked up her sweater, her face pinched and pale. "Just call me Batwings."

Kayla's cheeks flushed. "I meant to say *bird* wings, not bat wings. Even rather like a butterfly, the way they're formed in two sections. They're lovely."

"Yeah, right. I look like I stepped out of a horror movie with weird winged-aliens or something."

"That is so not true," Jade said, staring at Meghan. "They look perfect on you, and they have those nice green swirls on the edges. They're great, Meghan. Really."

"They *are* great," Kayla said, bobbing her head. "More than great—they're fantastic." She flashed an encouraging smile. "And they look wonderful. What I said came out all wrong. If I were you I'd march out there and—"

The door pushed open a crack. Kayla threw herself against it. "Jade, help!" she whispered hoarsely.

"We saw you go in there." It was Greta. "Open the door!"

Jade pressed her shoulder to the door as Meghan jammed her arms into her sweater. Her hands shook as she fastened the long row of buttons. She glanced at Jade and gave a tiny nod before yanking hard on the soft belt, tying it into a double knot.

Jade and Kayla stepped away from the door. It swung open, and Greta and two other girls stumbled into the locker room.

The second bell rang, the sound a long shriek echoing off the metal lockers.

"Showing your little buddies?"

"We were just leaving," Meghan said. "We're already late for class."

Greta's friends squared their shoulders and moved in front of Meghan, blocking her path.

Jade's eyes flashed. She took a step toward Greta. "Don't you have something else to do besides snoop around and spy on people?"

"I bet she doesn't even have wings," Greta said. "If she'd just take off that stupid sweater for a minute—"

"What are you going to do, force her?" Jade asked. "You know I'll kick that smile right off your face if you try it." She shifted into a taekwondo stance, hands raised, feet ready to strike.

Greta rolled her eyes. "Oh, now she's got a bodyguard."

"Make that two bodyguards," Kayla said. Her soft voice and elegant accent didn't sound the least bit fierce, but the look she gave Greta's friends convinced the girls to step back.

"What's the big deal?" Greta said. "All we wanted was to see her wings—if she even has any. Which I highly doubt." She sighed. "Just trying to get attention, I guess."

Meghan stared at Greta, but didn't say a word. *Nice try, but you're not going to trick me out of this sweater.* A shower dripped. The water ping-ping-pinged off the tiles. A straggler shuffled past in the hallway. No one spoke. Jade stood ready to strike, her eyes never leaving Greta's.

Greta's friend Nikki spoke up, a dark-haired girl with blue nail polish and a matching blue suede jacket. "Let's leave the queen bee and her drones," she said, "or do drones go with ants?"

Greta snickered, and took a few steps backward. "Who cares? They're both nasty insects." She yanked the door open. "Come on, we're out of here."

Jade shoved the door hard behind Greta and her friends. "It would be worth a suspension just to kick her—"

She glanced at Meghan, who had slumped onto one of the long benches near the lockers. Jade moved away from the door and strode across the small expanse of space between them. "Don't let her get to you," she said, and sat down next to Meghan.

Kayla nodded. "Who does she think she is—giving orders and expecting everyone to do her bidding. And what's with the gobs of makeup? She thinks she's classy, but it's more like trashy."

Meghan looked up, her face pale. "Thanks, but we all know she's gorgeous—with or without makeup. And everyone listens to her. She's probably saying what everybody else is thinking."

"Then show people your wings," Jade said. "There are laws about experimenting on humans, Meghan. Your grandfather may be freaking out at the moment, but this is a free country. No one can do things to you without your permission."

Meghan stood up from the bench. "You're probably right, but he still asked me to wait, lay low for a while."

"You're going to have to show people sooner or later."

"I will," Meghan said. "Later."

# CHAPTER NINE

# Squashed Bugs

T HE HOT LUNCH line was at least thirty kids long. Jade groaned. "It's going to take forever. I wish I was brown bagging like you."

"There's Kayla." Meghan tilted her head toward the slim girl with the silky brown hair, who stood with her back to them, halfway through the line.

Jade strode past the other kids in line and slipped in behind Kayla. "Thanks for saving me a place," Jade said. Kayla turned and grinned at her.

"You are *so* bad," Meghan whispered. She looked around the bustling cafeteria. "I'll find us a place to sit."

The jocks, clubs, and cliques had already claimed most of the tables. Meghan spotted an open section of seats—directly across from Danny. She swallowed, clutched her canvas lunch bag, and walked over.

"Howdy," she said. *Howdy? What happened to 'hello,' or good old 'hi'…I am such a dork!* She blinked and took a breath to steady her voice. "Are these seats saved?"

"Nope. All yours." Danny smiled at her. "Long time no see," he said, as she slid onto the bench on the other side of the table. Danny pushed the hair out of his eyes with the palm of his hand. He needed a haircut, but it looked good. Sun streaked and shaggy, like a surfer.

"Why is everyone saying you've got wings?" He craned his neck to get a better view of her back. "I don't see anything."

What should she say? Meghan's heart pounded so hard it made her stomach feel sick. She didn't want to lie, not to Danny. She fiddled with the zipper on her lunch bag and took a few quiet breaths, finally glancing up to meet his eyes. "They fold down really flat, like a fan."

"No way!" He sat up straighter. "Are you serious? I thought it was only a rumor."

In a whispered voice, Meghan told him about her winged ancestors. She couldn't mention magic, but she explained as honestly as she could that even though a lot of time had passed, somehow the genes she'd inherited had caused her to grow wings.

Danny flashed a dimpled grin. She had never really noticed the tiny gap between his front teeth. It was adorable. "Can I see?" he asked. "Why are you covering them up?"

"My grandfather wants me to keep it quiet, until he comes up with a plan. He's worried that scientists might try to do experiments on me." She glanced at the table next to them. A group of girls who'd been staring at her turned away and leaned together, heads practically touching, all talking at once.

"I won't say anything," Danny said softly. "But you must be going crazy. If I had wings I'd want to fly all the time."

Meghan looked up. Two of Danny's friends were heading their way, carrying hot lunch trays. "Uh, let's change the subject, okay?"

"So, what classes do you have after lunch?" Meghan asked, as his friends plunked their trays on the table and swung their legs over the bench. "I have Spanish, then World History. I think Science is after that."

"I had Science this morning with that new teacher, Mr. Wilson. He's cool, you'll like him. After lunch is Geography, and then Language Arts. World History's my last class."

*Just my luck. No classes together.*

"Hey, Dan-man," a tall boy called out. "When's our first practice?" He set his lunch tray in an open spot near the end of the long table. "I heard last year's starters can skip tryouts?"

Danny lifted his hand in a quick wave, and then turned back to Meghan. "I'm team captain for basketball this year. I guess I better go talk to him."

"Oh. That's great." She stared down at her lunch and let her hair swing forward, partially covering her face. "I mean, that's great about being team captain," she said, her words rushing out too fast. "Congratulations." She peeked up at him.

"Thanks," he said. A pink stripe streaked up each side of his neck and splashed onto his cheeks. "Coach asked me at the end of last year, but there are a lot of guys who play as good as I do, or better." He shrugged and stood up, cramming his half-eaten sandwich back into his lunch bag. "Anyway, I guess I'll see you around."

Meghan tried to smile, but her mouth wouldn't work right. "Yeah, see you around," she said, and poked through her lunch as if she was searching for something. She pulled out her water bottle and took a sip.

Danny's friends nodded at her and then scooted a few spaces down the bench to join some other boys. Meghan glanced in the direction of the hot lunch line. *What is taking Jade and Kayla so long?*

Greta's voice boomed above the chatter in the cafeteria. "I wonder what oversized insects eat for lunch?" Nikki and the other girls at her table snickered. "Probably something gross," Greta said, answering her own question, "like squashed bug sandwiches!" The girls squealed with laughter.

Meghan's face flushed hot. She blinked hard and tipped her water bottle up for a long drink.

Jade and Kayla made their way across the room with their lunch trays. Jade took one look at Meghan's face and said, "What's wrong?"

Meghan sighed. "Greta can't resist opening her big mouth, as usual. Right in front of everybody."

"She's just bent because Danny T was talking to you," Jade said. "I think she has a crush on him."

"Do you like him?" Kayla asked. "He's quite good-looking."

Meghan glanced at Danny. He was still talking to his friend. "Yeah, I like him. I mean not *like* him like him. We're just friends." She didn't mention that she agreed with Kayla about him being 'quite good-looking,' and she didn't add that she also thought he was smart. And nice. And his smile made her stomach feel tickly inside.

Meghan looked around the cafeteria. Everywhere she turned, kids were staring at her. Greta and her girls were laughing. Meghan took a bite of her sandwich and pretended not to notice. Grandpa had made her favorite—roast chicken, tomato, and avocado, with honey mustard and mayonnaise. She ate a few bites and put the rest back in her lunch bag. Too many knots in her stomach to eat the whole thing.

The hours crawled by until finally, the last bell rang. Meghan said goodbye to Jade and Kayla before starting the long trek home. A group of girls who lived near the school strolled along the sidewalk up ahead. One of them was Greta's friend, Nikki. Meghan slowed her pace.

The girls stopped walking and bowed their heads together, whispering, and glancing back at her. Nikki's shrill laugh rang out, and then one of the girls broke out of the huddle and yelled, "Why don't you *fly* home, Insect Girl?"

If only she could take off her stupid sweater, whip open her wings, and fly away! But she had promised Grandpa she'd wait. Meghan ignored the girls and bent over to rummage in her backpack.

"Why don't you use your *wings*?" Nikki shrieked.

The other girls laughed as if it was the most hilarious thing they'd ever heard. They started chanting: "Insect Girl! Insect Girl! Fly away, Insect Girl!"

Meghan grabbed her backpack and ran—she didn't even bother to zip it closed, just clutched it to her chest, crossed to the other side of the street, and ran as fast as she could. Nikki and the other girls soon faded behind her. Cars and houses turned into cows and pastures, but she kept running, pounding up the dirt road that curved through the hills.

Her gate was up ahead. She put on a last burst of speed and crashed into it, flinging it open. She yanked it shut with a clang and jogged up the long driveway to the house. Grandpa was outside raking leaves.

Meghan dropped her backpack and stood with her hands on her knees, gasping. Between gulps of air she said, "I'm – never – going – back – to – school!"

"What happened?" He leaned his rake against the side of the tool shed.

"I mean it, Grandpa. I'm not going back!" A whole sentence, squeezed out through ragged sobs. "I can be a home-schooler. I'll do all my work online."

Grandpa fished a clean handkerchief out of his pocket and handed it to her. "We'll talk about it." He gazed at her tear streaked face. "I'm guessing you didn't eat much at school today—I'll fix us something."

Meghan wiped her face with the handkerchief and followed him into the house. She slumped into a chair and watched as he sliced apples, pears, cheese, and brown bread, before piling it all onto a tray with two plates and two glasses.

He glanced at Meghan. "Bring the pitcher of lemonade, please. When life gives us lemons, right?"

Meghan didn't answer, but lemonade did sound good after her long run home.

Grandpa carried the tray outside to the table he'd built for their new lawn. It was their favorite place, right next to the roses. Meghan set the lemonade pitcher on the table.

For a couple of minutes, they just ate. Meghan was surprised she could even taste anything, much less think anything tasted good. But the silky pear slices were wonderful, and the thick bread with the sharp cheese and apple was exactly what she needed.

Finally, Meghan took a long drink of her lemonade and said, "Greta Von Stratton turned everyone against me, Grandpa. She said I eat squashed bugs for lunch." Fresh tears welled in Meghan's eyes. "My new name is Insect Girl."

"Now that's too bad." Grandpa frowned. "Sounds like her father has poisoned her against you."

"What are you talking about?"

He nudged the plate of food closer to Meghan. "Your mother and Dee Dee Von Stratton were friends from high school. Do you remember her? They brought you girls along to their art class."

Meghan nodded. "I remember. The teacher would always say, 'Here comes Dee Dee and Mimi and the mini-mes.'"

Grandpa smiled. "You little girls truly were mini-mes—cute as could be, and looked just like your mothers. Anyway, about a month after your mom left, Dee Dee moved to an art colony in California." He sighed. "After all these years, Robert Von Stratton still blames your mother—he thinks she encouraged his wife to leave him. Of course him being a sorry man to live with had nothing to do with it." Grandpa shook his head. "It's a shame he's brought his child into it. You two were sweet together."

"Well, she's not sweet anymore!" Meghan's voice was raspy from crying. "She's got everyone thinking I'm some kind of freak."

Grandpa reached for the lemonade pitcher and refilled her glass. "Greta probably wishes she had wings herself. She knows you're not a freak, you're the same bright, thoughtful girl you've always been. Maybe losing her mother turned her bitter."

"I lost my mom too, but I don't go around picking on other people." Meghan's face flushed. "Don't try to make me feel sorry for poor, motherless Greta! And you can forget about us being friends again."

"I never said you should be. What I'm saying is a person can have so much pain on the inside that it spills over to the outside." He paused, his gaze flickering toward town. "You hear about it on the news every day—people hurting other people, thinking maybe they'll feel better if someone else is suffering too."

Meghan nodded glumly, then glanced down to watch a butterfly land on the rim of her lemonade glass. It perched there for a moment before fluttering away. Other butterflies dipped low before passing by, as if they were saying hello.

"Being different isn't easy," Grandpa said. "Kids say cruel things—maybe they're jealous, or they're hurting inside and want to lash out. But if you're happy with yourself, it doesn't matter what others say." He took a long sip from his glass.

"I'm still glad I can fly, but how can I not care what people say? It's embarrassing, Grandpa." She gulped the rest of her lemonade and set her glass on the table with a loud *thunk*. "I can't *not* listen. I mean, I do have ears."

"Then walk away. Look at the butterflies. They're full of joy, but they're wise enough to fly away when there's trouble."

"Grandpa, you have no idea—even my own mother thinks I'm a freak."

"What in the world?" He put down his glass and stared at her. "What makes you think that?"

Meghan splashed a few inches of lemonade into her glass. "You called her *weeks* ago, when my wings first grew, but she never even called back. You said when she comes she can fix my shirts with the sewing machine. Not that I'm worried about my shirts, they're fine. I'm just saying—you called, and she's not here. It doesn't take a genius to figure out that she's not too thrilled about my wings."

"Now hold on a minute…I told you I left a message, but I never said anything about your wings. It was a company answering machine." He shook his head. "She doesn't know about your wings, darlin', and if she did, I think she'd be happy for you. It wouldn't change how she feels about you. She loves you."

"Whatever." Meghan's voice threatened another round of tears. "I still want to be home-schooled."

"If someone bothers you, walk away. If you're not there to listen they'll grow tired of talking to air."

"I'll walk away when they bother me in town—but please Grandpa, don't make me go back to school!"

Grandpa poured more lemonade in his glass. "You can ignore those mean kids," he said, "but you can't let them run you out of school."

Meghan pressed her lips together and turned away.

Grandpa sighed. "Robert Von Stratton's been saying rotten things about me for years, but that doesn't stop me from holding my head up and exhibiting at the fair. And who do you think gets hurt by hauling all that bitterness around?"

Meghan couldn't look at him. "A lot of kids do home-school. It's not that big a deal, Grandpa."

"McCoys don't let folks like the Von Strattons make decisions for us, darlin'. Staying away from school won't hurt anyone but your own self."

Meghan stared into the distance. "I wish my mom was here right now. She wouldn't make me go back. She'd understand."

Grandpa stiffened.

"Don't you see?" Meghan turned to him. "Everyone hates me, especially Greta. And everyone listens to Greta."

"How could anyone hate you?" Grandpa reached for a slice of pear. "The Von Stratton girl carries a load of heartache. Her harsh words aren't really about your wings, darlin'. How could they be? She's never seen them. She just enjoys aggravating you. It's wrong, but that's how she's handling her sorrow."

He layered a piece of cheese onto his pear slice and took a bite. "The best you can do is ignore her and go on with your life."

Meghan stood and picked up her plate and glass. "I'm going inside," she said, sighing. Home-schooling was out, at least for now.

••

EVERY DAY AFTER lunch, when they weren't fixing their hair or watching the boys play hacky sack in the center quad, Greta and her friends stared at Meghan, laughing, and whispering a little too loud. She knew they were talking about her—not that she ever heard her name, only "Insect Girl," or "The Insect."

Meghan never took off her long sweater, it became her uniform. If she didn't fly with Grandpa every morning, long before the sun came up—soaring and diving and twirling through the air—she would have wished her wings had never grown.

# Little Bird

M R. WILSON LEANED over the front lab table and poured black oil and blue tinted water into a beaker half-filled with sand. He stirred the contents with a rod.

"Greta," Mr. Wilson said, "please read the first question to the class and offer a hypothesis based on what you've observed."

"What, me?" Greta asked.

Mr. Wilson was tall and lanky, more like a cowboy than a science teacher, with dark wavy hair that brushed the top of his collar. Hazel-blue eyes peered intently under thick eyebrows. He held up a copy of the worksheet.

"But I didn't raise my hand." Greta bit her lip and slumped lower in her chair.

Jade's hand shot up, along with several other students' hands.

"I like to call on all my students, not just the ones who raise their hands. Question number one please."

Greta hunched over the page. In a halting voice, she slowly read the four sentences that made up the first question. Meghan's mouth almost dropped open as she watched Mr. Wilson coach Greta, stopping every few seconds to help her with the longer words.

He flashed her a reassuring smile. "Thank you, Greta. Now, what's your hypothesis?"

Kayla, who sat next to Meghan, shifted in her seat. "That was painful to watch," she whispered.

Meghan nodded. She'd always assumed Greta was a good student. Maybe her dad was too busy to help her with homework? Still, with all his money, he could hire a tutor. Meghan gazed at Greta, a twinge of sympathy flickering inside. After all, they were both motherless girls. And they used to be friends.

Greta glanced up. For a moment she looked like the little girl Meghan once knew, eyes wide and unguarded, pink flooding her cheeks.

••

SCHOOL DAYS FELL into a rhythm. Jade and Kayla's schedules were almost the same as Meghan's, she sat between them in most of her classes. Her other classes had a few girls she'd known since preschool—at least they didn't turn away if her eyes happened to meet theirs. And Danny smiled at her whenever they passed each other in the hallway…but most of her classmates ignored her. They weren't sure if her wings were weird, wonderful, or just a stupid rumor she'd kept alive by wearing her long, bulky sweater every day, even inside the warm building.

••

WINTER BREAK FINALLY arrived. Meghan joined Jade and Kayla at the craft store in town to buy supplies for making ornaments and gifts. They dipped green and gold wax candles, and shaped wire into silver stars and snowflakes to hang on their Christmas trees. Day after day they worked together, sitting at the long wooden table in Jade's dining room. Today Meghan was putting the finishing touches on Grandpa's gift.

"I wonder what Greta will give her dad for Christmas." Meghan frowned and repositioned a piece on the mobile she was making. Seashells, feathers, and chunky ceramic beads hung on fishing line, suspended from a smooth piece of driftwood. "My grandfather likes homemade gifts the best."

"It was easier when we were little," Jade said. "All we needed was crayons and markers. My parents got all misty-eyed over a picture I made of our family underneath a rainbow. They framed it—it's in the upstairs hallway. But I like doing crafts," she added, and held up her mobile for her friends to admire.

"I can't get mine to balance." Kayla moved a dangling seashell, which made her creation tilt in the opposite direction.

"Try this." Meghan handed her a shell from her own collection.

"Thanks!" Kayla tied the seashell onto her mobile. "I'd imagine Greta buys her dad cologne or an electric razor. She doesn't strike me as the creative type."

Meghan shrugged and dabbed a glob of glue onto her piece of driftwood. "Hard to tell," she said, and pressed a seashell into the glue. "Her mom is an artist."

"Really? Well, I'd wager Greta takes after her dad more than her mum." Kayla held up her mobile, now perfectly balanced. Meghan smiled.

"Nice!" Jade said. "I wish I could get mine to stop leaning sideways." She frowned and tied on another bead. "Greta's mom ran off and joined an art colony."

"Oh. That's a shame." Kayla tightened one of the knots that held a shell in place. "Everyone needs a mother…" She glanced up. "Meghan, I'm so sorry. I'm a perfect idiot."

"It's okay," Meghan said. "I'm used to it."

"Used to me being an idiot?"

Meghan shrugged. "No, used to not having a mother."

••

MIMI SENT A huge box of holiday chocolates, professionally wrapped, a point and click gift ordered online. Grandpa tried to call her, but there was no one at circus headquarters on Christmas Day.

"She must be out of the country," he said, as they set the table for Christmas dinner.

"I'm pretty sure they have phones in other countries." Meghan focused on folding their napkins into triangles, making each crease perfectly sharp. Grandpa glanced at her but didn't say anything. He lit the new green and gold Christmas candles, and poured sparkling apple cider into the crystal glasses, the ones they used for special occasions.

Grandpa had cooked way too much for just the two of them, a traditional feast right down to sweet potatoes with brown sugar and marshmallows, and homemade gravy for the turkey and mashed potatoes, not to mention homemade tangy red cranberry sauce—all Meghan's favorites. There were green beans with slivered almonds, and two kinds of pie for dessert, pumpkin and apple. Meghan wasn't really hungry, but she ended up eating everything on her plate, with a huge slice of pumpkin pie for dessert.

••

MEGHAN'S FAVORITE CLASS that winter was Science, where they were studying the life cycles of various animal species.

"It's very early in the season," Mr. Wilson said, "but there's a pair of Western Bluebirds nesting right outside our classroom." He pointed to a tall pine tree that grew next to the building. Everyone crowded around the window and looked up. A small hole was visible near the top of the trunk. "We won't be able to see inside the nest, but we can make deductions based on the birds' activities."

Classmates jostled each other to get a better view. "Look," Mr. Wilson said, gesturing to a blue and rust colored bird darting from branch to branch near the opening. "That's the male, protecting his territory."

Over the next few weeks, students took turns at the window, peering through binoculars and logging field notes while the rest of the class continued the lesson. Most days they spotted the male, usually with a piece of food dangling from his beak, ducking inside the hole to feed his mate. As the weeks passed they saw both parents carrying food—the eggs must have hatched.

••

On a clear blue Friday, a tall boy with glasses took his turn watching the birds. "Something fell out of the nest!"

Mr. Wilson rushed to the window and gazed through the binoculars, aiming at the grass beneath the tree. He beckoned the class to follow him outside.

The mother bird swooped and fluttered above a fuzzy blue-gray blob on the ground.

"It's one of the chicks." Mr. Wilson held up his hand to stop the students from pressing forward. The baby bird peeped and hopped as the mother bird fluttered around him. "Stay back, please. Let's not scare the mother away."

The mother bird swooped back and forth, her tweets growing more and more frantic. The chick peeped louder, but its hops grew weaker.

"Maybe Insect Girl can fly it up to the nest," Greta said.

Nikki nodded. "Poor little thing. Go on, Insect Girl. Fly it up to the nest."

Soon half the class was chanting: "Insect Girl can save it! Insect Girl can save it!"

"Stop that!" Mr. Wilson sounded more stern than Meghan had ever heard him. "Constructive, solution-finding ideas are welcome, but we *don't* call people names in my class."

Meghan couldn't smile her thanks or even look at him, her face felt too hot and twitchy. She watched as the mother bird darted to a low branch.

Mr. Wilson crouched down and took a closer look at the baby bird. "It doesn't seem to be injured. Looks like a mature nestling that's not quite ready to fledge, or we'd be seeing some short flights, or at least attempts." He glanced up, his gaze sweeping the circle of faces around him. "We can make a nest in a shoebox and feed it meal-worms, we still have plenty left over from last month's module. I'll get a box from the classroom, but hands off until I return, okay?"

Mr. Wilson motioned for Meghan to follow him. When they were out of earshot he said, "Don't feel pressured by your classmates. A chick that size will probably survive."

"Thanks," Meghan said, "but that bird belongs in its nest." The air seemed to rush out of her lungs and she had to take a few deep breaths. Finally she glanced up at Mr. Wilson and nodded. He gazed back at her, a half-smile on his face.

Everyone turned to look at her as she walked back to the circle. Only the little bird's peeping broke the silence. "My name is *not* Insect Girl," Meghan said. Her voice shook a little, but her words were clear. "My name is Meghan Michaela McCoy-Lee."

A silent thrill rippled through the students as Meghan untied the belt on her mother's old sweater. No one moved—they barely even blinked.

Meghan shrugged off the sweater and in one swift, fluid movement, she flicked open her wings. They gleamed in the sunlight.

Her classmates gasped. Mr. Wilson called out, "People! Please step back—she needs some space."

Moving slowly, Meghan lifted the baby bird and cradled it in her cupped hands. With a powerful push off the ground, she flapped hard and soared up to a thick branch near the nest. "You belong here little bird," she said, peeking into the opening and tucking the tiny creature next to another one inside. The mother bird perched nearby, her head cocked to the side.

Meghan gazed down at her classmates far below. *Amazing, Awesome*, and *Cool* floated up on the breeze. She drank in the sound of their words.

With a gentle push off the tree, she flapped a few times and then glided down to the grass. Her classmates surged forward and gathered around her, everyone talking and asking questions, all of them smiling.

"I suspected the rumors might be true," Mr. Wilson said, his eyes shining. "That was an incredible rescue. Wow."

Greta pushed through the crowd. "That was amazing," she said. "And your wings aren't actually hideous after all."

"Thanks, I guess."

Greta stared at the ground and rocked back and forth. "Sorry." She glanced at Meghan. "I meant to say your wings are pretty cool." She smiled politely, like they were meeting for the first time.

Meghan smiled back. Truce. It was better than all-out war.

"Here." Greta held out Mimi's sweater. "I picked it up for you."

Meghan took the sweater, but she didn't put it on.

••

WHEN THE LAST bell rang, Meghan stuffed the sweater into her backpack and slung the strap over one shoulder. The sun warmed her wings, folded against her back.

Her classmates surrounded her, still jabbering and calling out questions. Other students rushed to join the throng, spilling off the sidewalk and into the street. Drivers cruised by at a careful crawl, curious about the commotion.

Meghan nodded and smiled and answered as many questions as she could, considering she couldn't mention anything about butterflies or magic words.

"Hey Meghan!" a voice called. Meghan turned around. It was Danny, running to catch up. She waited, suddenly shy.

He stared at her wings, wide-eyed and grinning. "Very cool. You're so lucky!"

"Thanks," Meghan said. They stood there smiling at each other while a few dozen classmates milled around them, snapping photos of Meghan and her wings.

Danny's gaze flickered away. "Isn't that your grandfather?"

Grandpa strode up to them, red-faced and huffing. He leaned forward with his hands on his knees, trying to catch his breath. He nodded to Danny, then raised an eyebrow at Meghan.

"Grandpa, this is Danny Taylor."

Danny smiled at him and shook hands.

"Well, it looks like you had an interesting day," Grandpa said, turning to Meghan. His voice sounded strained. "I'm sorry to pull you away from your friends, but we need to talk."

"I have to go," Meghan said. With a wave to Danny and the other kids, she let Grandpa steer her away. "I'm sorry, Grandpa. I had to help a little bird that fell out of its nest and—"

"It's all right, darlin'. I couldn't keep you covered up forever. We'll stick to our story about genes and leave out the rest, and hope for the best." He wrapped his arm around her shoulders as they walked. "I was planning to contact someone soon, just hadn't fixed my mind on who that person should be. I was thinking maybe a professor from the university—but whoever we told, sooner or later it would have leaked out to the news media."

He winked at her, but he looked worried. "You beat me to it, someone from your school must have called the TV stations. I didn't answer the door, stayed real quiet until they gave up, then I snuck through the forest and came out behind your friend Lena's place." He stopped and wiped his face with his handkerchief. "They're all down at the gate now, waiting."

Meghan tugged on his arm. "Uh, I don't think they're waiting by the gate anymore," she said, as a line of news vans rounded the corner and cruised in their direction. The vans sped up, and then screeched to a halt. Reporters poured out and rushed at Meghan, surrounding her and barking questions.

A reporter grabbed the edge of Meghan's wing. He stared into a camera and said, "The surface is quite smooth, with a flexible, leather-like texture."

"Let me go!" Meghan cried.

Grandpa shoved him, hard, and the man let go and staggered back—but he didn't stop talking. "Give her some room!" Grandpa moved in front of Meghan, blocking the reporter's view.

"We're not trying to hurt her," one of the other reporters said. "We just want to see what her wings feel like." Fingers reached from behind, brushing and squeezing the edges of Meghan's wings. She pulled away, but they pinched harder.

Meghan whirled around. "Leave me alone!" She closed her wings tight against her back.

"You can't go grabbing people's kids!" Grandpa shouted, and the reporters eased off a little. Grandpa took a deep breath and eyed the faces surrounding them. "Now if you can behave yourselves, we'll answer your questions in an orderly manner."

The reporters rushed forward again, shouting questions and waving microphones.

"Enough!" Grandpa roared. "You've lost your chance." He pulled Meghan close and whispered, "You know, you don't have to put up with their shenanigans."

A slow smile spread across Meghan's face.

"Whenever you're ready," he said. "No time like the present."

# CHAPTER ELEVEN

# The Knock at the Door

MEGHAN FLUNG HER wings open, which made the reporters jump back. She flapped hard and lifted off. Grandpa caught up to her, holding his jacket, with his wings jutting out through slits in his shirt.

"They can see your wings!" Meghan cried.

He grinned. "It's about time!"

A reporter shouted, "The old man's got wings too!"

"Watch what old looks like!" Grandpa shouted back.

They dove and twirled and zoomed through the sky, with the news crews running back and forth beneath them. The reporters kept crashing into each other, their eyes on the sky instead of their surroundings. Meghan and Grandpa laughed so hard their cheeks hurt.

"I'm running out of breath," Meghan squealed, as a cameraman bumped into a parked car. He stopped to rub his eye and took a moment to get his camera pointed at them again.

Grandpa chuckled. "Silly fools! I reckon it's time to tell our story, but not to these hooligans. Let's get them off our trail." He pressed forward, slanting skyward until a thermal updraft surged under their wings, pushing them to a higher altitude. They were harder to spot now, two small specks in the blue. A line of news vans moved along the street like ants, trying to follow them.

Meghan and Grandpa circled wide toward home, dipping down to glide on the current that ran through the hills before flapping hard to crest the steep hill beneath their house.

A few reporters leaned against the gate, others sat inside open vans parked on the side of the road. They looked up in astonishment as the two flyers swooped over their vans. Cameramen grabbed equipment and charged for the gate.

Meghan landed near the kitchen door with Grandpa close behind her. They dashed inside.

"Phew!" Meghan turned the deadbolt. "That was close." She poured a glass of water for herself and offered one to Grandpa.

*Knock! Knock! Knock!*

Grandpa gulped down his water and peered out the window. Meghan stood behind him, craning her neck to see past his shoulder. Reporters and cameramen crowded onto the front porch, red-faced and panting from running up the hill.

*Knock! Knock! Knock!*

Grandpa opened the door but held his hand up, palm out. "All right," he said. "We hear you." He scanned the faces in front of him. "Reckon you can sort yourselves out and pick one of you to do the talking? I'm not inviting all of you into my house."

"Mr. McCoy," said a white-haired reporter, "how about just the networks? That would cut it down to three of us, plus our camera crews."

A tall reporter with a deep tan and designer sunglasses called out, "Hey! Who put you in charge?" He unclipped his i.d. badge and waved it at Grandpa. "Mr. McCoy, me and my crew got here half an hour before the networks even showed up."

"Not my problem," Grandpa said. "I'm not having a mob inside my house—pick one of you, take it or leave it."

The reporters and their cameramen swarmed forward, bumping into each other on the small front porch, a few getting jostled off the porch and onto the grass. "Mr. McCoy! Mr. McCoy!"

"Hold on, now." Grandpa took a step backward, his eyes flashing. "Enough of this nonsense. Which one of you got here first?"

A friendly looking woman in a dark blue suit called out, "That would be me, Sir." She waved her hand high above her head. Grandpa beckoned her forward and she began weaving through the knot of reporters and cameramen.

"What's your name, young lady?"

"It's Amanda Clark, Sir. Channel Seven. 'News and weather on the hour, every hour.' The station next to the clock tower, right here in Apple Creek."

"Well, come on in, then." Grandpa gave her a tense smile and held the door open a little wider. "Leave your camera crew for now. Maybe we'll take some pictures later."

She looked over her shoulder at the crowd of newsmen. "Email my office and I'll send all of you a copy." She winked at the white-haired reporter. "I'll even send one to you networks." She squeezed past Grandpa and into the house. Meghan smiled at her.

"Now I'm closing this door," Grandpa said, "and the rest of you will kindly step away. This here's private property—if you're not back at the gate in two minutes I'm calling the police." The news crews grumbled and turned away, trudging slowly toward the gate.

Amanda Clark looked around the cozy living room, admiring the paintings and fine old glassware from Ireland. After a few minutes, Grandpa led her into the kitchen and pulled out a chair for her.

She smiled and said, "Ready to get started?"

Grandpa nodded. "Ready or not, right?" He winked at Meghan.

Amanda clicked on a small recorder. "Have you always had wings, Mr. McCoy?"

Grandpa told her about the early McCoys who were born with wings, and that his own wings grew when he was the same age as Meghan—perhaps the new growth had something to do with puberty, all the changes in the body...

Meghan's face flushed with warmth. *Please, Grandpa! Do you have to talk about puberty?* But she had to admit that it sounded logical.

The reporter turned to Meghan. "Did you have to learn how to use your wings, or did it come naturally? Any close encounters with planes up there?"

While Meghan answered her questions, Grandpa slipped into the living room and pulled out the family photo album. He pushed *The McCoy Family Register* further back on the shelf, out of sight.

"This is absolutely amazing!" Amanda said, turning the pages of the album. "It must be some kind of genetic aberration. I've never seen anything like it."

Grandpa's face froze. "I'm not sure I understand your meaning, Ms. Clark." He picked up the photo album and tucked it under his arm. "Our family has been blessed with wings, we are not 'aberrant.' If you're going to talk about us like we're freaks—"

"I'm so sorry, Mr. McCoy! Aberration was a poor choice of words." She smiled at him, her voice polite and sincere. "What I meant was a family trait that's way outside the norm."

He nodded and set the photo album back on the table.

She turned to Meghan and said, "I'd love to have my own pair of wings. Flying must be fantastic!"

Grandpa allowed her to bring her van up to the house, with a cameraman to film Meghan flying around the garden. Meghan performed her most complex rolls and spirals. It felt good not to hide her wings anymore. And flying in the middle of the day, with blue sky all around her? It felt wonderful.

"One final question, Sir. Why have you kept your own wings hidden all these years?"

Grandpa's smile shut down. "A man has a right to his privacy." He swept his hand toward the crowd gathered along the fence and at the gate. "And now, if you don't mind," he said, ushering Amanda and her cameraman back to their van, "we've had enough talking for today."

Meghan stared out the window and watched Amanda's cameraman latch the gate behind him before climbing back into the van. Grandpa came up beside her. Meghan had the feeling he liked Amanda, for a reporter.

Meghan's stomach rumbled a long, loud growl.

Grandpa grinned at her. "You hungry?"

Meghan laughed. "Starving!" She opened the fridge.

"It's way past supper time." Grandpa rummaged through the freezer. "How about veggie lasagna?"

"Mmm, I love your lasagna. I'll pick some lettuce and tomatoes for a salad."

She peeked outside. Reporters leaned against the gate in the twilight, and camera crews lounged by the vans, smoking cigarettes and talking. "Be right back," she said, and quietly cracked the door open enough to squeeze through.

Shadows blanketed the garden. Meghan crept forward, padding on bare feet toward the concealment of the corn patch—

The evening exploded! Cameras flashed, and shouted questions flew through the air like rapid-fire bullets. Meghan spun around and sprinted for the kitchen door. She locked it behind her.

Grandpa unwrapped the foil from the lasagna. "That rabble can't see past the front of our property, unless they trespass and come up the hill." He slid the pan into the oven. "You'll be fine, once you're inside the garden."

"But what if one of them is already up here? Someone could be hiding behind a tree, ready to jump out and take my picture." She opened the fridge and dug through the crisper drawer. "I guess I'll make squash instead."

She was sick of summer squash—they'd harvested endless bushels of it, enough to share with the food bank in town. She washed it anyway, and then turned to Grandpa. "What that reporter asked about your wings…why the big secret? I mean, why did you hide them from me?"

Grandpa sighed. "I wish I could have told you a long time ago. It's been a hard secret to keep." He opened the cupboard and pulled out two plates. "Remember when Bitsy died? You were heartbroken over that little hamster." He set the plates on the table. "I saw you crying over her little grave the next day. I had to stop myself from coming out to hug you—but you would have wondered what was hanging on my back."

He shook his head. "And let me tell you, it got mighty hot in the summertime, wearing an extra shirt to cover my wings. When you were in school I just kept one handy, nearby. Not that I didn't appreciate your help all those summers …"

"I guess I got used to seeing you that way, you know, like sun protection. But I can't believe you didn't trust me—I wouldn't have told anyone."

Grandpa nodded. "I know that darlin', and I do trust you. But I gave your mother my word."

Meghan's eyes narrowed. "What does this have to do with my mom?"

"Your mom firmly believed that my wings would confuse you, or create some kind of problem for you." He sighed. "She's your mother—I had to respect her wishes."

He turned and began filling a pitcher with water from the faucet. "But I figured it didn't much matter anymore, once you grew wings of your own." He set the pitcher on the table, along with two glasses. "Now, how about getting that squash in the steamer. I'm talked out for tonight."

"Please, Grandpa, why didn't she want me to see your wings? I mean, why would it confuse me? I don't understand."

"I don't fully understand it either, darlin'. You'll have to ask her when she gets here."

"Right," Meghan said. "Whenever that is." Suddenly she felt very tired. *Why do we keep pretending she's coming home someday?*

# Not Another Reporter

MEGHAN WOKE THE next morning to the sound of voices. *Not another reporter!* She burrowed under the covers. She needed time to think about everything that had happened.

Grandpa said something she couldn't make out, and the other voice, a woman, laughed.

Meghan hurled the covers off. She knew that laugh! She ran into the kitchen.

"Mom!"

"Meghan! Look at you! You've grown so much."

Meghan walked into her mother's outstretched arms and held on tight. They stood there, swaying slightly, until Meghan finally let go and stepped back. Her mother looked different now, not as rosy and soft as she remembered. Same gold flecked green eyes, but she was leaner, her skin a light tan, and she'd let her hair grow out to the middle of her back.

Tears welled up and ran down Meghan's cheeks. They were both crying now, Mimi softly and Meghan in great drenching sobs. She had six years of tears waiting to come out, there was no way to hold them back a second longer.

Meghan buried her face in her mother's embrace and drew in deep, gulping breaths. The warm scent of orange spice filled her lungs and wrapped around her heart until her sobs quieted into soft hiccups.

Grandpa wiped his eyes with the back of his hand. "Why don't you give me your backpack," he said, helping her mother out of a small ostrich-leather pack. "You got some luggage in the car?" Mimi nodded. "Best plan on staying a while," Grandpa said, smiling. "I don't think she'll let you out of her sight anytime soon."

He handed Meghan his handkerchief. "No more tears now—this is a happy occasion! You two go on out to the garden and I'll bring us some breakfast. Who wants pancakes?"

"I do!" Meghan said. "Come on, Mom." She grasped Mimi's hand. *Mom.* It felt so good to say that word. Mom, Mom, Mom. *Mom* is back!

••

Meghan led her mother to the table near the roses. A breeze rustled the leaves, and the morning sun beamed warm rays onto the garden.

"There's something I need to tell you," Mimi said. "Or maybe I should show you." She turned around and shrugged the sweater off her slender shoulders. Folded against her back were two shiny wings, each bottom section tucked neatly underneath the top. She flicked her wings open.

"Mom!" Meghan gasped. "You're just like me!"

Mimi laughed. *Nobody* had a laugh like her mother's.

"Yes, sweetheart, I'm just like you." Her face turned serious. "That's why I stayed away all these years. I wanted to tell you, but I didn't want to…how can I explain this?" She paused, searching for the right words. "I didn't want to decide your future for you."

"What are you talking about?" Meghan pulled out a chair and sat down.

"When you were a little girl," Mimi said, sliding into the chair next to Meghan, "you followed me everywhere, copied everything I did. Do you remember?"

"Of course I remember."

A flicker of grief crossed Mimi's face. "When your dad died everything changed." She pressed her lips tightly together before breathing out a long sigh. "The house we loved seemed strange and lonely. We couldn't go on living there. That's when we moved in with Grandpa."

"But why did you move away?" Meghan swallowed hard.

"I'm so sorry, Meghan," her mother said. "I'll try to make it up to you."

Meghan blinked, squeezing her eyes closed for a moment. "Just tell me why you left," she said. "And please, don't leave anything out."

Her mother took a deep breath. "Okay," she said. "That's fair. You deserve to know everything."

She stared out past the fields terraced beneath the garden. "Your grandpa had wings long before I was born. He never hid them from me, but I knew not to tell anyone." Mimi turned to look at Meghan. "Part of me wanted to grow wings like his, but part of me didn't. When I was your age I got as far as reading the magic words, but I never said them out loud. I was glad I hadn't done it. I wanted to be normal, like other girls."

*I wouldn't exactly call myself 'abnormal.' Different maybe, but not abnormal.*

"So, how did you get your wings?" Meghan asked. "And when?"

"I grew them after your dad died, the same way you did." Her mother's cheeks dimpled in a quick smile. "I wished hard and said the magic words. And I had a little help from the butterflies."

Meghan glanced toward the house. She remembered her conversation with Grandpa about her mom not wanting wings—when she was Meghan's age. *Talk about fancy footwork, Grandpa.* He never mentioned that she grew them later!

"You won't remember because you were still a baby," her mother said, "but when your grandmother died, Grandpa was pretty torn up. He couldn't eat, couldn't sleep—puttered around the garden, hardly went out to the fields. We didn't have much of a harvest that year."

"Wow. That doesn't sound like Grandpa."

Her mother nodded. "Then he started taking long flights to clear his mind. It helped him, brought back his spark. Years later, when your dad died, I felt so lost…it was a sadness beyond anything I could ever imagine. That's when I began to think about flying. I thought it might help me, and for a while, it did."

Her mother shifted in her chair, turning toward the forest and the steep mountainside rising out of the trees. "I flew through the trees and up the side of that mountain almost every morning while you were at school. There's a beautiful waterfall there, very secluded. It was my refuge during that time. I'll take you there someday."

She turned back and waved a hand in the direction of the gate. Flashes of light glinted in the air—the sun reflecting off dozens of camera lenses from the news crews hidden beneath the rise of the hill. "Your grandpa never wanted to deal with this," she said. "You know how he likes his privacy."

Meghan began picking at a loose hangnail on her thumb. She glanced up at her mother. "But I still don't understand why you left."

"I couldn't keep hiding my wings from you," Mimi said. "We shared your room, remember?" A memory floated across Meghan's mind: two beds, side by side, in what was now her room.

Her mother stared at her, watching her face. "I had no choice, Meghan. I had to go. Sooner or later you would have accidentally seen my wings, or felt them on my back. You loved to copy me, sweetie. You would have begged me to let you grow wings too."

"Well, you didn't have to tell me how to get them!" The words snapped out—she didn't mean for her voice to sound so angry, but it did. "You can't grow wings if you don't know the magic words. I was six. You could have made me wait until I was older."

Her mother winced. "Don't you think I've thought about all of this? Leaving you broke my heart. But I didn't want to influence you. If you saw my wings you'd want your own, even if you had to wait a few years—and poof!" She waved her hand, like smoke rising through the air. "There would go your chance to decide for yourself." She sighed. "I was only trying to protect you."

Meghan leaned back and tried to let the words sink in. *She was only trying to protect me.* She took a deep breath. *Only trying to protect me.* Another breath, the words hushing through her mind like a mantra. *Trying to protect me.* She focused on a wren darting from branch to branch until her heartbeat slowed to a quiet thump.

Her mother hadn't taken her eyes off Meghan's face. "How could I visit for a few hours and then leave? There was no way to explain that to you. I needed to stay away until you were old enough to decide for yourself."

*And I needed a mother.* "I really missed you," Meghan said.

Her mother's smile was positively radiant. "Well, we're together now. And look at us! You could be my younger twin, everything about us is exactly alike—even our wings." She stood and opened her arms wide.

Meghan hugged her, and then pulled away, flicking her wings open. "I love having wings," she said, looking over her shoulder. Her wings shimmered softly in the sunlight. "But I'm still learning how to glide into a landing. Hovering is easier." She settled back into her chair and gently rubbed her scuffed knees.

Her mother smiled, but it didn't quite reach her eyes. She brushed off the rose petals that had drifted onto her chair and sat down again. "Grandpa told me about your flying dreams, sweetie. If I had known you would want wings on your own, without trying to copy me or your grandfather…" Her shoulders sagged. "I could have shown you my wings a long time ago," she said, her voice dropping to a hoarse whisper. "It wouldn't have made a difference."

Meghan's heart lurched with a sickening thump. She had wanted wings ever since she was a little girl—long before her flying dreams. When she and Jade were kindergarteners, they played a game called 'Fairy Princess' where they dressed up in Jade's mom's fancy old bridesmaid dresses—and pretended they could fly.

*If only I had told my mom about our game… I already wanted wings! She didn't need to hide hers from me. She didn't need to move away.*

A cold, heavy weight settled inside Meghan's chest, pressing against her heart. *It's all my fault.*

Grandpa cleared his throat behind them before setting a tray of pancakes on the table. "Fiddlesticks! I forgot the forks."

"I'll get them!" Meghan was already on her feet, eager to think about something other than all the years she and her mother had lost.

Meghan jogged along the path to the kitchen door. She grabbed the forks and turned around, taking a shortcut back, her mind deep in thought, walking quietly between two rows of corn before coming out on the far side of the green bean frames.

Grandpa's voice rang out. "Absolutely not!"

Meghan stopped and listened.

"Okay, Dad. I'm just thinking out loud. She's old enough now—"

"You already decided what's right for her," Grandpa said. "That hasn't changed."

"Well, maybe it has. Meghan's growing up. She's old enough to decide for herself."

Meghan stepped out from the edge of the green bean frames. "Decide what?" She walked up to them.

"Oh, we have plenty of time to talk about everything." Her mother took the forks from her and set them on the table. "Let's eat these pancakes while they're still hot."

Meghan turned to Grandpa. "What?" she said. "Decide about what?" She sat down in the chair across from him.

"It can wait." He slid a stack of pancakes onto her plate.

Meghan glanced back and forth between Mimi and Grandpa. *Not now.* She didn't want to do anything that might upset her mother.

"Fine," Meghan said, and she pulled her plate closer.

# Mr. Black Baseball Cap

"I'LL NEED A place to sleep. Is it okay if I share your room for a few months?"

Meghan smiled. "That would be great!"

Mimi scrolled through her phone. "I'll order a futon—it will be a nice little couch for your room, but it can unfold and turn into a bed for while I'm here."

The futon arrived later that afternoon. Mimi hummed softly as she and Meghan smoothed a spare set of sheets and blankets onto the futon's sleeping pad. Two beds, side by side, the way it used to be.

At bedtime Mimi asked, "Can I tuck you in, or are you too big for that?"

Meghan gazed up at her mother. "It's okay. I'm not too big."

Mimi leaned over the bed and snugged the quilt around Meghan's shoulders. Meghan closed her eyes and breathed in her mother's fragrance. Her whole body felt light with happiness, but there was a lump in her throat like she might cry.

"Goodnight, Mom," she whispered, blinking her eyes open for a moment.

Her mother smiled. "Sweet dreams, Meghan."

••

THE NETWORKS KEPT calling and sending letters, and Grandpa finally agreed to an interview with CMN. A reporter flew in from New York. His camera crew set up portable studio lights in a conference room at Chateau Pomme, Apple Creek's oldest and finest hotel.

The reporter was waiting for them in the hotel lobby. "You brought your granddaughter! Will she be taking part in our interview today?" He shook Meghan's hand.

"No. It's just me, like we agreed." Grandpa rested his arm across Meghan's shoulders. "She wanted to come along and see how you make your TV show."

The reporter led them down a wide hallway, their footsteps muffled by thick carpet. Elegant statues stood in lighted niches, and oil paintings lined the walls. As they passed the hotel's small, glass-walled exercise room, Grandpa ducked inside to take a drink from the water fountain on the other side of the open door.

The reporter leaned close to Meghan's ear and said, "I bet you'd like to be on TV." His white teeth gleamed when he smiled. "Think you can talk some sense into your grandfather?"

Meghan's stomach twitched. It would be different if she had a script, like in a movie. But an interview was risky—what if she said the wrong thing, revealed too much? Her throat went dry. "It's okay," she said. "I'll just watch."

Grandpa walked up to them and they continued down the hallway. "I appreciate you being right on time," the reporter said. "We should be able to get started in a few minutes." He stopped outside a pair of double doors and opened one side with a key. A hubbub of chatter flooded out as cameramen and lighting and sound technicians adjusted equipment and bustled through the large room.

Meghan looked around for a place where she could sit and watch the show without getting in the way of the production crew. She stepped over a mass of cables criss-crossing the floor and squeezed past a box of extension cords, before perching cross-legged on top of a plastic crate that had been flipped over and pushed against the wall.

"Right here, Mr. McCoy." The reporter gestured to one of the two sleek leather chairs in the center of the room. Grandpa settled into the chair and waited, staring straight ahead.

A man carrying a clipboard shut the door. "Quiet on the set!" he called. The room fell silent. "Lights!" Two studio lights turned on, reflecting off the shiny leather chairs. Grandpa squinted and blinked. The reporter slid into the seat across from him.

"Cameras rolling!" called the man with the clipboard. "In 5, 4, 3, 2, 1!"

The reporter smiled into the camera. "Welcome to CMN Spotlight! Joining me today is Michael McCoy." He turned to Grandpa. "We're delighted that you've agreed to spend some time with us."

Grandpa smiled and nodded his head.

"Your family has been in the news quite a bit lately, a media sensation. Wings on human beings—it's almost mythical, like something out of Greek legend."

Grandpa grinned. "Well, I'm no legend, but it is a wonderful thing. Me and my girls enjoy flying. It's a real treat."

They chatted back and forth for a few minutes. Meghan smiled. *Grandpa almost looks relaxed. This reporter is really nice.*

The reporter cleared his throat. "Having wings must be great fun." He cocked his head to the side and leaned forward. "But have you considered the contribution you could make to science?"

"What are you talking about?" Grandpa asked, his voice dropping low.

"Mr. McCoy, you may be able to solve one of the world's greatest mysteries—the origin of mankind." The reporter beckoned to someone off camera.

A woman in a light green uniform stepped out from the shadows in the far corner of the room. She held a small metal tray with a hypodermic needle and several glass vials.

"We've brought in a licensed nurse from the Institute of Genealogy—"

*No!* Meghan sucked in a breath and held it.

"What's going on here?" Grandpa was halfway out of his chair, his gaze darting wildly around the room. He took the handkerchief out of his pocket and wiped his forehead.

"Your genes could be the missing piece of the puzzle, evidence of a link to another species. Perhaps man is related to birds, not apes."

"What? I'm not related to birds, or apes! The good Lord made me human, like you." Grandpa's face turned blotchy red. "I didn't come here to be treated like a lab rat."

"Mr. McCoy, I assure you, it's a simple blood test." The reporter paused. "You could go down in history as the man who cracked the code, the source of humanity right there in your DNA."

Grandpa leaned back in his chair. "So, if a man's born with webbed hands or feet, he's related to a duck? Or maybe a frog?"

The reporter frowned, his lips pressed together in a thin line.

Meghan crept closer to get a better view of Grandpa's face. Their eyes met for a moment. He winked at her, then turned back to the reporter.

"I heard about a person who was born with a tail. I reckon he might be related to a cat or a dog. Or maybe a donkey." Grandpa's eyes flickered to the reporter's waist as if he expected the tip of a tail to peek over the top of his belt.

The reporter raised his hands. "Okay, let's not debate evolution." His lips curled, but his eyes weren't smiling. "Sometimes genes are influenced by environmental factors, such as genes for diabetes that are activated by eating too much sugar. Can you think of anything that may have activated your family's flying genes?"

*Right, like he's going to tell you about our family book and the butterflies.* Meghan held her breath. *Be careful, Grandpa.*

"Your letter said you were going to interview me about *flying*—our fastest speed and highest altitude…" Grandpa squinted and wiped his face with his handkerchief again.

The show aired later that evening. By the time they finished watching it, the vein above Grandpa's jaw pulsed in an angry beat. He clicked off the TV. "That man had me squirming like a schoolboy in the principal's office. Made it look like I was hiding something."

Mimi smiled at him. "You handled him really well, Dad. You just have to get used to talking in front of the camera."

Grandpa's eyebrows drew together. "Why do I have to get used to it? We don't owe these people. No law says we even got to talk to them."

••

THE NEXT MORNING, Meghan heard the crunch of tires coming up the gravel driveway.

She ran to the window. A white van had pulled up next to Grandpa's truck. The door slid open and a cameraman climbed out. Stepping down from the driver's seat was Amanda Clark, the friendly young reporter who had first interviewed them.

Grandpa's blue-gray eyes stared straight into the camera. "This here is a statement for the news media. Me and my family are not giving any more interviews. And we'd appreciate if you'd stop calling us on the phone and shouting questions when we're trying to do our business. If I got something to say I'll call Amanda Clark from Channel Seven News, like I did here today. The rest of you can move on now. No sense wasting your time. If any of you news people get within ten feet of me or my girls, we'll fly away."

When the camera turned off, Amanda asked, "Do you honestly think the media is going to stay away? Reporters are tenacious—I should know."

"Oh, I expect they'll keep at us," Grandpa said. "But I'm giving them fair warning. All they'll get is closed mouths, and flapping wings." He shrugged. "They're bound to give up sooner or later."

"So, don't call us, we'll call you?" Her eyes twinkled, and the smile she was holding back turned into a grin.

Grandpa laughed. "You got it. And you'll be the one I call—if I call anyone. But I wouldn't be waiting by the phone if I was you."

"You're really something, Mr. McCoy." She shook her head. "You know, most people enjoy being in the spotlight."

Grandpa wiggled his wings up and down. "Well, Ms. Clark," he said, the corners of his eyes crinkling into a smile, "as you can plainly see, I'm not most people." With that, Grandpa hoisted one of the equipment bags and walked Amanda Clark and her cameraman back to their van.

..

EXCEPT FOR THE news crews that still hung around the gate, life returned to normal. Well, almost normal.

"Will you look at that!" Her mother pointed to a huge black and chrome pickup truck parked outside the grocery store. A freshly painted sign gleamed on the side of the truck: *Von Stratton Farms, Apple Creek, Oregon… Taste the magic!* A little girl with sparkly wings flew over a field of crops, sprinkling magic dust.

Meghan gasped. "She looks like me! Maybe a few years younger, but her hair is almost the same, even the shape of her wings is the same. The only thing different is my wings don't sparkle."

Mimi stared at the sign, shaking her head. "He's got a lot of nerve. What a rip-off! He has no right to use a flying girl for his advertising. The only one who has that right is your grandpa." She leaned close to Meghan's ear and whispered, "Not that your grandpa would ever use the word 'magic,' even if people think it's just an expression. I'll talk to him about it. Maybe we'll sue and get the sign removed."

As they wheeled a shopping cart toward the entrance, the double doors slid open. Robert Von Stratton came out, pushing a grocery cart loaded with cases of soda and beer.

"Well, lookee here. It's my long-lost friend, Mimi Lee."

"Hello, Robert." Her mother's voice sounded flat. "Nice sign you got there." She nodded toward his truck.

Behind him, a shopper frowned, tapping her toes and waiting for them to clear the front of the doorway.

"Uh, Mom?"

Her mother and Mr. Von Stratton glared at each other, neither one moving. Meghan grabbed the edge of her mother's cart and tugged it sideways to let the shopper pass. Mr. Von Stratton pushed past them without another word.

*Well that was awkward…*

Mimi pressed her lips together and watched him walk away. She shook her head, and then pulled a piece of paper out of her purse before steering the cart through the doorway. "Let's not forget your grandpa's list—oats, vanilla, chocolate chips…sounds like he's making oatmeal cookies."

"Mom?" Meghan asked. "Did you really tell Dee Dee Von Stratton to leave Mr. Von Stratton?"

"Is that what he's been telling people? That man is a—"

"No! He never even talks about it," that she knew of anyway. "It's just, well, Grandpa told me he blames you."

Mimi frowned, a red flush had crept up her neck and onto her cheeks. "Dee Dee was one of my closest friends, Meghan. I never said anything that wasn't already on her mind. Robert is lucky she stuck it out for so many years. He treated her like dirt." She grabbed a box of muffin mix off a display. "And he hasn't changed a bit—still a complete jerk."

They strolled slowly through the aisles, deciding what they wanted as they went along. At the dairy aisle, Meghan read the items on Grandpa's list. "We need cheese, yogurt, sour cream, and low-fat organic milk." Her mother winked and added a carton of chocolate milk before turning toward the checkout line.

Meghan nudged her and pointed to a tabloid headline: *Angels or Aliens? The Mysterious McCoys!* Mimi giggled and pointed to another one: *The Real McCoy or a Hoax? Whole Family Flies!*

As they wheeled their grocery cart out the exit, Meghan tugged on her mother's arm to make her stop. "Look who's waiting for us," she said. Four reporters and four cameramen stood next to Mimi's car. "They must have followed us here."

Her mother shrugged and pushed forward. "Hi, fellas!" She gave them a dazzling smile. "You know the rules, no interviews."

Passersby craned their necks to see why the newsmen were in the parking lot. Her mother waved, and then turned to the cluster of reporters. "Sorry guys. It's his house, his rules. No talking to the media."

"Hello, Meghan! Nice to see you with your feet on the ground." A young man reached out his microphone. "Feel like talking today?"

Meghan smiled at him but shook her head. She recognized him. He was one of the reporters who had waited in front of her school every day after her wings first grew. He always waved at her and made her laugh with his comical begging gestures, instead of yelling like some of the others when she flew over their heads—and landed out of sight inside the center quad.

"Come on, Ms. Lee, just one or two questions." A tall reporter jabbed a microphone toward her mother. He wore a black baseball cap with his shirt and tie, and black high-top sneakers.

He was the same reporter who had tried to interview them last Saturday when they went out for breakfast with Grandpa, practically pouncing on them as they walked out of the restaurant. Meghan had disliked him instantly.

"Can't a man have a simple meal with his family?" Grandpa had said.

"How about a photo with the three of you flying? Or stand together near the restaurant—a casual family outing. Our readers will love it."

"I'll thank you to leave us in peace." Grandpa's eyes narrowed. "I told all you news people—we're done giving interviews. We weren't put on this earth to satisfy your curiosity. Now go on with you and report some real news."

"Mr. McCoy, people want to know about you and your family. Just answer a few questions and I'll get out of your hair."

"Keep walking." Grandpa curled his arm around Mimi's waist and gently prodded her along. Meghan held onto his other arm.

The reporter scrambled in front of them, zigzagging back and forth, firing questions. "Seen any UFOs up there? Has the Air Force or NASA contacted you?"

Grandpa held onto Meghan and her mother and pressed forward.

The reporter dropped back and came alongside Mimi. "Ms. Lee, what about you and Meghan? Any plans for Hollywood?"

"I asked you politely." The vein in Grandpa's neck popped out. "Now stand aside and stop bothering us."

"Just answer one or two questions and I'll be happy to oblige, Mr. McCoy."

"I'll not have the likes of you telling me what to do!" For a moment it looked like Grandpa was going to lunge at him. He took a deep breath instead, and turned to Meghan and Mimi, glancing upward with a subtle jerk of his chin. In one fluid motion, he shrugged off his jacket and whipped open his wings.

Meghan and Mimi zipped out of their jackets. Up they flapped, a half wing-stroke behind Grandpa, leaving the reporter far behind.

Now here he was again, Mr. Black Baseball Cap, but no Grandpa.

# A Name from the Past

THREE MORE REPORTERS sprinted across the grocery store's parking lot. Word had leaked out that Meghan and her mother were out in public without Mr. McCoy, and the news teams flocked to them like hungry seagulls. In a matter of minutes their ranks swelled from eight to eighteen, and now two more news vans were driving toward them.

They were trapped—with so many reporters crowding them, there wasn't enough room to take off. Meghan glanced at her mother.

Mimi was smiling like a queen greeting her subjects.

Meghan sucked in air, but it didn't seem to fill her lungs. Her mother was radiant, calm. *She is enjoying this!*

Mr. Black Baseball Cap's face twisted in a wheedling smile. "Come on, just give us a few words." He leaned in close and held the microphone near Mimi's face. "What are your plans, Ms. Lee? Staying here with us in Apple Creek?"

The others pressed closer, waving their microphones. Cameramen shouted, "Over here! Ms. Lee! Meghan! Give us a smile."

Meghan backed away, but bumped into someone behind her. Two hands groped along the outside of her shirt, squeezing her wings so hard that she gasped. She whirled around the other way, but there was nowhere to go.

She grabbed her mother's arm. "Mom! They're scaring me."

As Mimi turned to look at her, a tall, muscular man came into sight, jogging across the parking lot. He wore a tan button-down shirt and a dark green tie—the grocery store's colors.

"Mimi!" he called. "Are these guys bothering you?" He elbowed through the throng and came to her mother's side, towering over her like a brown-haired, blue-eyed fortress.

Meghan read the name badge clipped to his pocket: *Brian Richards. How do I know that name?*

Her mother smiled up at him. "Hello, Brian. I was wondering when I'd run into you."

The reporter with the black baseball cap turned to his cameraman. "Are you getting this?"

Brian glared at him. "You were just leaving, right?"

"No law against us being here." He signaled to his cameraman. "Keep rolling. Get whatever you can."

Brian gripped the handle of Mimi's shopping cart and turned to face the mob of reporters. "I suggest you move out of the way." He pushed the cart back and forth like he was taking aim with a battering ram, ready to make a path if the reporters didn't move.

They moved.

Meghan grasped the side of the shopping cart and held her mother's wrist with her other hand, with the reporters trailing behind them, still shouting out questions. Brian let go of the cart for a moment and turned around, squaring his shoulders and scowling at the mob. "Don't even think about following us into the store," he said. "I'll have you arrested for causing a public nuisance."

Meghan and her mother glanced at each other and smiled. "A hero, just when we needed one," Mimi said, as she hurried to keep up with Brian's long strides.

"Who is he?" Meghan whispered. "I recognize his name."

"He was a good friend of your dad's—they were on the football team together. I haven't seen him since the funeral."

Brian beckoned to one of the baggers as they entered the store. "Please put Ms. Lee's groceries in my office." He handed over their shopping cart and smiled at Mimi. "Let's get you and Meghan out of here." He nodded toward a small alcove next to the customer service desk.

They followed Brian up the narrow stairway at the back of the alcove. The top of the stairs ended in a large, rectangular room. Meghan squinted as her eyes adjusted to the fluorescent lights.

Brian looked at his watch. "We should have the break room to ourselves for a while."

"Thank you for rescuing us." Mimi smiled at him and settled into one of the white plastic chairs.

He nodded. "That's what friends are for."

Meghan walked over to the long window that looked over the store. "Is this how you catch shoplifters?"

Brian joined her at the window. "Don't tell anyone, but most of them don't stay caught. A stolen candy bar or a package of cheese is a high price to pay for a criminal record."

"You mean you let them go?"

"If it's kids they have to sweat it out in my office until their parents pick them up. Adults get a stern warning, and the phone number for the food bank." He shrugged, and his handsome face softened into a smile. "My rule is one mistake per customer. Try it again and I call the police, no more Mr. Nice Guy."

Meghan smiled back at him. He really was a nice guy.

He moved away from the viewing window. "What would you like, Meghan? Soda, or a bottle of water?" He pressed a handful of coins into the drink machine.

"Thanks!" Meghan pushed the button for Sprite.

Brian turned to her mother. "What about you, Mimi?"

She glanced up at him and shook her head.

"Come on, let me get you a drink. We can wait them out up here."

"What if they don't leave?" her mother said. "They're used to waiting around for hours. My dad's rule is to fly away anytime they try to talk to us, but how am I supposed to fly with a cartload of groceries?" She raised her eyebrows, looking back and forth from Brian to Meghan. "Maybe I should go down and give them a statement this one time, so they'll go away?"

Brian shook his head. "I think your dad may have the right idea. It's like a dog who begs at the table—ignore him and he'll give up, but give him a taste and he'll never stop pestering you." He smiled at her. "Not that I'm trying to tell you what to do."

Her mother sighed. "I don't *know* what to do. I just want to get our bags home before the ice cream melts."

"I can put your cold items in one of the refrigerators in the stockroom." Brian held out his hand. "Give me your keys—I'll deliver your car and your groceries when I get off work in a few hours, and your dad can drive me back. If you and Meghan fly off the loading dock where the deliveries come in, no one will even know you've left the store."

"Brilliant!" Mimi said. "You were always so smart in school, Brian. I should have known you'd come up with a plan."

Brian rocked back on his feet and stared at a point past her mother's head. "If you'd like, maybe *you* can drive me back. We could stop and get a bite to eat, catch up." The blood rushed to his face. "For old times' sake, old friends—no disrespect to David."

"It's okay, Brian. David's been gone a long time. He'd be glad we ran into each other."

Brian nodded. "Meghan is welcome to join us, if she'd like."

"Uh, that's okay." Meghan glanced sideways at her mom, whose cheeks had flushed pink. "I mean, thanks, but I have a bunch of stuff to do."

Mimi took a deep breath and looked up at Brian with her best smile. "All right, then," she said. "I guess it's a date."

# Flirting with a Beemoc

"FOLLOW ME," BRIAN said, "and try to blend in." He turned and gazed at Mimi. "Not that you could blend in anywhere—still as gorgeous as you were in high school."

Meghan caught the look her mother gave him and swallowed a smile. *You little flirt. I knew you were starting to like him.*

They paused in the cereal aisle and examined a few labels, as if they were shopping. Brian turned at the end of the aisle and headed for the meat department. Beside it was a pair of swinging double doors. He glanced over each shoulder, and then pushed open the doors to a cavernous stockroom stacked with crates of green bananas, flats of shampoo, cases of conditioner and toothpaste—all ready for the night crew to restock the shelves.

Brian pointed to a wide steel door on the other side of the stockroom. "The loading dock is straight ahead."

••

"BYE BRIAN, THANKS again!" Meghan hovered twenty feet above the loading platform.

She waved as a trucker stacking boxes on the next platform stopped to stare up at her, then she turned away to watch her mother and Brian say goodbye.

They were laughing. Brian leaned his head closer to her mother's ear and said something. She smiled, gave him a quick hug, and stepped back to flutter into the air.

Meghan and her mother flew low until they were out of sight of any reporters still hanging around the store's parking lot. "I saw how you sparked up around Brian," Meghan said. "What's the story with you two?"

"Well, he's an old friend…we share a lot of memories from high school." She glanced sideways at Meghan as they flew. "Would you rather I not go out with him? I think your dad would want me to have a life, don't you?"

"I'm totally fine with it, Mom. Brian seems like a great guy." She grinned at her mother. "Not to mention he's really cute, too."

Her mother laughed. "He's too old to be cute, but he's definitely easy on the eyes."

"So, he was a friend of Dad's?"

"They were the Beemocs, hung out together all the time."

"What are Beemocs?" Meghan asked. "Is that a club or something?"

"Not really a club," her mother answered. "More of a group. It stands for Big Men On Campus – B.M.O.C., the popular guys."

"Were you popular too?"

Her mother's smile faded. "I guess you could say that. But I never felt like I fit in, not really. At least, not on the inside."

··

Grandpa was reading on the bench beneath the giant oak tree. He closed his book when Meghan plopped down next to him. "How was the shopping?" he asked. "Did you get your grandpa some good treats? Maybe a lollipop or a chocolate bar?" He grinned and held out his hand. "I'll settle for some jellybeans, if that's all you've got."

Meghan laughed. "Sorry, Grandpa, they weren't on the list. But I did have a soda while we were there." She told him about meeting Brian.

"Brian Richards. I see him in town from time to time. He and your dad were close, even after high school. Does it bother you, your mom going on a date with him?"

"Of course not. He's nice, and it's not like she's old or something."

"Hey, what does being old have to do with it? Maybe I want to go on a date too." He gazed at her, chuckling.

"Grandpa, be serious. Mom's only thirty-one. Lots of people her age get married again."

Grandpa stopped chuckling. "It would be a fine thing for your mother to find love again."

"Oh, Grandpa, *wouldn't* it be? Then maybe she'd want to stay here forever." Meghan slumped against his side and leaned her head on his shoulder.

"Well, from what you told me, it sounds like he's pretty sweet on her."

"Do you think they'll fall in love?" Meghan asked. "How long does it take?"

Grandpa rested his hand on hers for a moment. "That's a hard question to answer, darlin'. It can take weeks, months, even years. For me and your grandma it started with a 'meant to be' feeling. Only your mother and Brian will know if that's happening for them. I hope so. We'll have to wait and see."

She sat up straight. "I almost forgot, we saw Mr. Von Stratton at the grocery store. There's a picture of a flying girl on the side of his truck. Can you believe it?"

Grandpa nodded. "I spoke with him about it last week— saw him at the hardware store. It's his new logo."

"That's it? You're going to let him get away with it? The girl looks like me, and everyone knows Apple Creek is where we live. He's acting like we're connected somehow."

Grandpa shrugged. "Well now, Robert Von Stratton lives in Apple Creek too. We might even call him a neigh- bor, seeing as how we live in the same town. And the little girl resembles you, but she's not identical. I think we can let this go."

"Well, he could have asked us first. And anyway, why are we being so nice to him? I thought you hated Mr. Von Stratton."

"I never said that." Grandpa leaned forward on the bench, his eyes locked with hers for a moment. "It takes a lot of energy to hate a person. We only get one turn on this earth, and I'm not wasting mine carrying a load of hate on my back."

"But it's not right, acting like we're related to him or something—anyone but the Von Strattons!"

Grandpa sighed. "I can't say I'm liking the association, but it is what it is. And I thought you and his girl were friends again."

"She acts like we are, and I know I'm supposed to forgive her and all that, but it's hard to forget how mean she was before." Meghan shrugged. "I don't really trust her."

"I'm glad you're not enemies anymore," Grandpa said, nodding, "but it's wise to be cautious when someone's done you wrong." He cleared his throat. "Her father rankles me, but it won't hurt us to share the glory."

"But Grandpa, people will think we gave him permission."

Grandpa stared out past the edge of the hill to the fields terraced below. "Nothing on his logo says 'McCoy,' so no one can rightly say we gave him permission." He paused and gazed at her stormy face. "We need to be generous with him, darlin'. Robert Von Stratton truly believes our family is responsible for his loneliness."

"Do you think my mom really did convince Greta's mom to leave?"

Grandpa shook his head. "I suspect he'd find the main reason in his own mirror—but your mom might have encouraged her. Those ladies spent a lot of time together doing their art work. I suppose they shared their sorrows, the way friends do."

"Then they must have talked about leaving their families."

"I'm not so sure about that. Now, Greta's mom may have planned to leave, but I don't think your mother did." He paused and glanced toward the house. Mimi was still inside. "It was an impulse she had, not something she thought all the way through—when the circus came to town, something about it spoke to her, seemed to solve the things that were bothering her."

"Yeah, I guess she thought she needed to protect me from finding out about her wings." Meghan took a deep breath, trying to push down the sick feeling that rose in her stomach. If only she had told her mom about playing Fairy Princess with Jade! She could have shown Meghan her wings instead of running away to join the circus.

"Did Greta's dad know about Dee Dee's plans?" Meghan asked, glancing up at Grandpa. "I mean, did he try to stop her? Maybe he would have been nicer to her, if he knew."

"No telling what was going on behind closed doors. All we know is Dee Dee lost hope, felt like she couldn't go on being married." He paused and gazed in the direction of town, a wide, hazy patch in the distance. "Robert Von Stratton is a hard man, but who knows? Maybe they could have stayed together. But when your mom struck out on her own, well, you might say it gave Dee Dee the confidence to do the same thing."

Meghan nodded. "Now I understand why Greta hates me."

Grandpa wrapped his arm around her shoulders. "Your mom never set out to harm anyone, least of all little Greta. Her parents are adults, they're responsible for their own selves." He glanced down at her. "The flying girl picture on his truck might give Robert's business an extra boost." He gave her shoulder a squeeze. "If it helps even the score in his mind, then it's all right by me."

••

*RING, RING! RING, ring!*

Grandpa unplugged the phone mid-ring and turned to her mother. "Mary Margaret, please leave the phone unplugged. I'm ready to throw that blasted thing out with the trash."

"It's Mimi, Dad. Everyone calls me Mimi." She smiled at Grandpa and shook her head, like he was acting ridiculous. "How will I know if someone needs to reach me? What if Brian's trying to call?"

Grandpa's expression eased. "He can always call you on your cell." Grandpa looped the cord around the phone and tied it into a knot. "A man can't think with all the noise around here."

Every day the mailbox overflowed with letters from agents, talk show hosts, and television producers. One letter proposed a reality show, another offered a book deal. Grandpa tore up the letters and threw them away. Mimi dug them out of the recycling bin and taped them back together.

"Why not let me and Meghan do a few shows?" Mimi sighed loudly and planted her hands on her hips. "It's not a secret anymore."

"And the McCoys are not a bunch of freaks parading around for people to gawk at. We're the same as we've always been, except now people know we got wings. The less fuss we make, the sooner we can get back to our lives."

"You're so old fashioned!"

But Grandpa wouldn't budge.

With no more interviews and nothing new to write about, the news crews finally left the front gate. The reporter with the black baseball cap snapped a few pictures of Mimi and Brian holding hands, with headlines like *On the Wings of Love* and *Love Birds at the Park,* but everyone else moved on to other stories.

••

THE DAYS GREW warmer. Summer was just around the bend. On the last day of school, Meghan and her friends followed their classmates into the library media center. Colorful streamers draped the main desk, and the tables were decorated with yellow or blue paper tablecloths, the school's colors. Students chatted at their tables or milled around the room, holding plates piled high with treats.

"Hey Meghan," Danny said, stopping by her table and holding up a cookie that shimmered with sparkly sprinkles. "Did you make these?"

Meghan smiled. "Me and my mom did." Her mother had found angel, bird, and butterfly shaped cookie cutters.

"They're really good!" Danny cocked his head to the side and tossed back the shaggy hair that had flopped onto his forehead.

"Thanks," Meghan said, smiling.

"Well, uh…" His hair flopped forward again. He pushed it back with his free hand. "Maybe I'll see you this summer." He stood there for a moment like he was about to say something else. "Okay, well, I guess I'll catch you later." He turned and hurried away.

Jade leaned closer to Meghan's ear and whispered, "I think he likes you."

"No way! We're just friends." Meghan tugged on Jade's arm. "Stop staring at him! He'll think we're talking about him."

Meghan glanced around. Greta had snagged Danny's arm and was playfully stealing his cookies. "He always hangs out with Greta—he obviously doesn't like me. Did you see how fast he left?"

"Duh. That's because he feels shy around you." Jade grinned at her. "Which is because he likes you."

Kayla crossed the room with a cup of punch in her hand. "What are you two talking about?"

"Danny T," Jade whispered. "He likes Meghan."

Meghan shushed her friends with a look.

"Don't worry, no one can hear us," Jade said. The room hummed with laughter and conversation.

"Do you really think he likes me?" Meghan whispered. "He hardly even notices me."

Kayla's gaze flickered to Danny. "Oh, he definitely notices you," Kayla whispered, barely moving her lips. She turned back to Meghan. "He was staring at you."

Meghan shifted her head to casually glance in his direction. Now he and Greta were pretend fighting over a brownie she had stolen off his plate. Greta was laughing hysterically.

Meghan sighed. "He's an old friend. Everyone knows he likes Greta. Just because he happened to look over here doesn't mean anything."

The last bell rang. The class cheered, then rushed to stuff their trash into the bins.

The librarian smiled and opened the door. "Have a wonderful summer!"

Summer—no more waking up early, no more homework, and no more tests! It also meant no friends. Jade was leaving day after tomorrow for her cousin's house in Portland—she'd be gone almost a whole month. And

Kayla's family would be leaving soon to visit relatives in Europe.

Meghan walked outside with Jade and Kayla. They sat on the grass under the shade of a clump of trees, talking and watching their classmates stream along the front sidewalk until the last few students straggled out of the building carrying art projects and musical instruments.

Jade sighed. "I better get going. My mom will wonder what's taking me so long."

"Me too," Kayla said.

"Me three."

They laughed a little. It softened the sadness of saying goodbye.

# Queen Greta

FLYING HOME, MEGHAN spotted a lone figure trudging up the hill.

"Greta!" she called as she glided down to earth. "What are you doing?"

"I was looking for you, genius. No one else lives this far from school." Greta wiped her forehead on her shirt. "You're lucky you can fly. This hill is steep, and *hot*."

"I know, I used to walk it every day. There's not much shade." Meghan eyed the shadow cast by a pile of giant boulders further up the hill, but rattlesnakes like rocks—better hot than dead.

She slung her backpack over one shoulder and studied Greta's face. Strands of hair stuck to the sides of her cheeks in damp clumps, and beads of sweat pearled across her forehead.

"I thought I'd try to catch you on your way home. You were with your friends after the party." Greta glanced over her shoulder toward their school. "I told Nikki and the other girls to meet me at the soccer field. Some of the guys are playing football…"

"Danny plays football, right?"

"Yeah, Danny and his friends. Actually, that's what I came to talk to you about."

Meghan shifted her backpack onto her other shoulder. It really was hot out.

"I see you two talking sometimes…" Greta shrugged. "I was wondering if maybe you like him."

Meghan's heart sped up. "Well, of course I like him. Danny's an old friend."

"You know what I mean." She locked eyes with Meghan. "He's been a friend of mine since we were little kids." Pink blotches bloomed on Greta's neck and cheeks. "But it's more than that now."

Meghan was tempted to fly straight home and leave Greta standing by herself in the hot sun. Like that would accomplish anything. She sighed. "It's no one else's business who I do or don't like."

Greta snorted, holding back a laugh. "It's pretty obvious, Meghan. You were all flirty and smiley around him at the party today."

"I wasn't flirting! He's a friend, we talk. And anyway, I bet half the girls in the class like him."

Greta glanced upward with a help-me expression. "He only cares about you as a *friend*, Meghan. He's just being nice." Greta gathered her long hair and lifted it off her neck. "In case you didn't notice, he's that way with everybody." She shrugged. "I'm trying to save you from embarrassing yourself. You're going to look like an idiot if you keep following him around."

Meghan's jaw tensed. "I don't 'follow him around'— I have *never* followed him around. And anyway, I'm not one of your entourage who does whatever Queen Greta tells them to do."

Greta's face turned a deeper shade of pink. "Everyone knows he likes me. It's common knowledge."

Meghan stood up straighter and held Greta's gaze. "It's a free country. I can be friends with anyone I want. And I'm not going to stop talking to him! I've known him since preschool."

"That's not what I—"

Meghan held up her hand. "I finally figured out what you've had against me all this time. I mean, until these last few months. You've actually been pretty nice lately."

"What are you talking about? I don't have anything against you."

Meghan took a deep breath. "You think my mom talked your mom into leaving," she said in rush. "Maybe my mom did encourage her. If she did, I'm really sorry. I know how it feels to not have a mother around."

Greta's mouth dropped open. "What? At least my mom isn't a circus act!" She shook her head. "Our mothers have nothing to do with this, Meghan. All I'm saying is Danny already likes me. A friend would respect that, if you know what I mean."

*Seriously?* Meghan stared at the ground, scratching lines with the heel of her shoe onto the crumbly dirt road. *I'd hardly call us friends…more like frenemies.*

Greta sighed. "I didn't mean to say that about your mother."

"Yeah." Meghan dug her heel deeper into the dirt, carving out a tic-tac-toe grid.

"I'm trying to apologize here." Greta watched her, waiting for her to look up. "It really would be cool to hang out together." She bent down and wiped her face on the hem of her shirt. "If you want, you can sit with me and my friends at lunch next year."

Meghan glanced up. "I already have friends, thanks."

"I guess they can sit with us too. No big deal. The more the merrier, right?" She laughed. "Kayla's got a little style, and Jade's all right, as long as she's not giving me one of her *looks*."

Meghan paused, searching for words. "Uh, no offence, but I doubt they'd be interested in sitting with your friends."

Greta's eyes flashed. "In case you haven't figured this out, being famous doesn't make you popular, Meghan, it just makes you well known." She took a deep breath, her lips curving into a smile. "Think how much fun next year will be if you're in my group." She smiled bigger, but it didn't quite reach her eyes. "We pretty much rule A.C.M.S."

Meghan wiped her damp forehead with the palm of her hand. "Thanks for the invitation. Anything else?"

"No, that's it."

Meghan's heart pounded. "Did Danny tell you he likes you?"

"He doesn't have to say it. Everybody knows he does." Her eyes scanned Meghan's face. "Well, *almost* everybody."

The air quivered with heat. Meghan took a breath to steady her voice. "If you're worried about me and Danny, then you kind of wasted your time coming all the way out here. I always help my grandfather in the summer. And my mom's here too. She'll want me to do stuff with her." Meghan focused on a point past Greta's shoulder. "I have other things to do besides chase after a guy."

Greta's lips pressed together for a moment, suppressing a grin. "Whatever, Meghan. Have a good summer." She lifted her hand in a small wave and headed back down the hill toward their school. She was practically skipping.

Meghan groaned. *Did I just tell her she'll have Danny to herself all summer?*

••

Mimi was waiting for Meghan in the kitchen.

"Hurray! Summer's here!" She linked arms with Meghan and twirled around. Meghan shuffled her feet, but her heart wasn't in it. She was still thinking about Greta, replaying their conversation in her mind.

"Hey, what's up with the down face?" Mimi asked. She let go of Meghan's arm. "It's the first day of summer! Think of all that freedom stretching out in front of you."

Meghan shrugged, and grabbed a peach yogurt out of the fridge. "I guess I'm just tired," she said, and slumped into a chair. She peeled the lid off the container and swirled listless circles with her spoon.

Mimi nodded. "Tired, and maybe something else? Is it a boy problem? You know you can tell me anything. That's what moms are for."

No way was she telling her mother about Danny. What was there to tell? Greta would be hanging out with him all summer, end of story. She glanced up. "It's just that I'll miss my friends. Jade's going to her cousin's for almost a month, and Kayla's family is traveling."

She plunked her yogurt container on the table and sat cross-legged on the floor, unloading her backpack into 'keep' and 'throw away' piles.

Mimi reached out and ruffled Meghan's hair. "It's summer, sweetie. The best time of the year."

Meghan looked up from the books and papers stacked around her on the floor. Her backpack was empty. The school year was officially over.

Her mother smiled down at her. "You and I will be so busy having fun, you won't have time to miss your friends. I promise, you're going to have a great summer!"

••

THE DAYS HUMMED along with a cheerful rhythm. Every morning before the sun got too hot, they harvested plump melons and loaded them into Grandpa's truck. Mimi turned everything into a game, and they chatted and laughed while they worked. And Grandpa seemed to smile all the time now, when he wasn't cracking jokes or singing old songs.

In the afternoons, when Grandpa took his nap, Meghan and Mimi flew to the mountains behind Grandpa's house, where they both acted like little kids, playing hide-and-seek, and tag, chasing each other around the tops of tall pine trees. Afterward, they'd cool off in the mist of her mom's special waterfall or relax on the smooth rocks that ringed the icy pool, reading books and snacking in the shade of the scattered trees. They soared home on the evening breeze, the golden glow of sunset on their wings.

Meghan was happy. Very happy. And her mom seemed happy too. Mimi met Brian in town for dinner once or twice a week, and on the weekends Meghan joined them at the movies, or they strolled together through town, stopping at one of the little cafes for lunch, or for a picnic in the park.

••

"I FEEL LIKE a teenager who can't make up her mind." A pile of clothes was heaped on the futon. Mimi held up two sleeveless blouses. "Help me decide—green, or peach?"

"Go with the green one, it makes your eyes look even greener." Meghan folded a stack of shirts and put them back in the drawer. "I think you've tried on everything you own, and most of my stuff, too." She grinned at her mother. "I can tell you really like him."

Mimi breathed a happy little laugh. "What's not to like?" She pulled the green blouse over her head. "He's one terrific guy." She looked in the mirror and twirled to see herself from every angle, a soft, dreamy smile on her face. She seemed to glow with quiet excitement.

*She's falling in love!* Meghan smiled. *Looks like it's meant to be.*

# CHAPTER SEVENTEEN

# Spyin' on Brian

JADE CALLED—SHE was finally home from her cousin's house in Portland.

"I can drop you off on my way to the hardware store," Grandpa said. "Just be back before seven."

"But it's summer, Grandpa. It won't be dark until nine." Meghan finished the last bite of her sandwich and gave the lid of the peanut butter jar an extra twist. "You wouldn't have to worry about me if I had my own phone." She tried to smile, but it came out wobbly.

"How's a phone going to help you fly at night? You take a wrong turn and don't see a pole or the side of a barn—wham!" He clapped his hands together.

Meghan sighed. "Grandpa, everyone my age has their own phone."

"And they play games and text their friends when they should be doing homework."

"You know I wouldn't do that. And it's summer—no homework!"

"If you want privacy we can put a phone jack in your room." The corners of his eyes crinkled in a smile. "I'll pick one up while I'm in town. That way you can talk in your room whenever you like."

"But if I had a cell phone I could talk wherever I was, not just in my room." She drank the rest of her milk and set the empty glass in the sink. "Everyone at school has their own phone."

"Everyone?" He raised an eyebrow.

Meghan's voice rose in frustration. "Well, everyone except me and Jade—her family can't afford one. And maybe a few others."

Grandpa grabbed his keys off the hook by the door. "Talk to me about it in another year or two." He looked over his shoulder. "You coming?"

"This is so lame." Meghan groaned and followed Grandpa as he headed for his truck. "It's like living in the Stone Age."

Grandpa chuckled. But Meghan wasn't smiling.

••

A WEEK LATER, Kayla returned from her trip to the UK. The three girls had agreed to meet in front of the library, and after they'd hugged each other and settled onto the wide steps to talk, Kayla said, "I've got drinks for us." She unzipped the outside pocket of a new leather backpack and pulled out three Cokes.

"Thanks!" Meghan popped open the top and took a long swallow. "Mmm—mine has bits of ice in it." She peeked inside the can.

Kayla smiled. "I put them in the icebox so they'd still be cold when I got here."

"I think we call that a 'freezer.'" Jade's eyes twinkled in a smile. "Welcome back to America."

The girls finished their sodas and walked inside. They browsed the titles on the shelves, pointing out the ones they'd already read, and choosing new ones. Within an hour each girl had a tall stack of books ready to check out.

Meghan began sorting through her books, thinking about her long flight home. *Maybe I'll save some of these for next time.*

"Isn't that your mom's friend?" Jade asked, interrupting her thoughts. A dark-haired man wearing bike shorts stood at the information desk. An empty-looking drawstring backpack hung from his shoulders.

Meghan ducked. "Quick, don't let him see us!"

Jade and Kayla crouched beside her. "Why are we hiding?" Jade whispered.

"I don't want him to think we're spying on him," Meghan said, speaking in a hushed voice.

Kayla covered her mouth with her hand to stifle a laugh. "It's not like we followed him here," she whispered. "We're checking out books. That's what people do at the library."

Meghan gestured toward the back rows. "I just don't want him to see me." They slipped behind the shelves and worked their way to the furthest corner of the library, *The Reading Nook*.

Meghan sank into a beanbag chair. "Will one of you do me a favor?" she whispered. "Go to the information desk and ask a question—maybe you can hear what he says to the librarian. Or follow him and see what he's checking out."

Jade plopped down on an overstuffed chair and swung her feet onto the footrest. "I knew it! We *are* spying."

Meghan smiled. "I just want to find out why he's here. Maybe I can clue my mom in about stuff he's interested in."

"I'll go," Kayla said. "We shop at the grocery store by our house. He's never even seen me."

Kayla wove around the back of the library, and then strolled toward the center desk. Both librarians were busy. She stood behind Brian and waited.

Meghan and Jade crept closer and peeked around the side of the shelves. "He's taking a long time," Jade whispered. "Seems like he's asking a lot of questions—maybe he's working on some kind of project."

The librarian finished writing, smiled at Brian, and handed him a slip of paper. He nodded, then turned and began walking toward the back corner.

Meghan gasped. "He's coming this way!" They headed for the opposite corner. "Just act normal," she said, tugging on Jade's shirt. "Slow down. He'll notice us for sure if we look suspicious."

The two girls stopped in the young adult section and glanced through the titles. Meghan poked her head out at the end of the row. Brian was leafing through the pages of a book and walking slowly toward *The Reading Nook.*

Someone tapped her on the shoulder. Meghan swallowed a yelp and whirled around.

"I've been searching all over for you," Kayla whispered. "I was about to check the loo—I mean, the restroom."

"We almost got caught," Jade whispered. "We had to move."

Meghan raised her eyebrows and pointed at a closed door with a sign above it: *Study Room.* She peeked inside the thick glass panel. Jade and Kayla came up behind her. "No one's in there," Meghan whispered. "And it's soundproof."

They settled into seats around the small table. "So, what was he checking out?" she asked.

Kayla smiled. "Cookbooks. *Romantic* cookbooks."

"Romantic *cookbooks?*"

"I couldn't hear everything," Kayla said. "But I definitely heard the librarian say '*Dinner a Deux,*' and '*Romance and Ravioli.*' I think she was flirting with him a bit. He's terribly handsome. Your mum is lucky."

Meghan smiled. "He's super nice, too. But what does 'a deux' mean?"

"Deux means two in French," Kayla answered.

"I guess he's planning to cook for her," Jade said. "Sounds serious to me." She grinned at Meghan.

"And that's not all." Kayla looked back and forth from Jade to Meghan. "He asked where the parenting section is, and if there's a book she could recommend for step-parents."

"Wow!" Meghan said. "He's seriously getting serious."

Kayla smiled. "If he marries your mum, you'll have a really great stepdad."

"I bet he's planning to wrap a ring in ravioli and pop the question," Jade said. "Soft music, candles, a romantic dinner—he's going to propose!"

Kayla looked worried. "I hope she doesn't swallow the ring!"

Meghan laughed. "I'm sure he'll find a way to warn her without ruining the surprise."

..

Summer was more than halfway over, the days were going by too fast. Meghan stretched and rolled over in bed. It seemed late, and the house was awfully quiet. Her mom and Grandpa must be outside working.

She grabbed her robe and padded into the kitchen. Mimi sat at the table, drinking coffee and flipping through the pages of a fashion magazine. A long, gold box decorated with a red velvet ribbon rested on the seat beside her.

Mimi looked up and smiled. "For you." She handed the box to Meghan.

"But it's not my birthday."

"Not yet," her mother said. "But soon. And it's not actually a birthday present. Go ahead and open it."

Meghan slid into the chair across from Mimi and slowly untied the ribbon. Inside the box laid a satin gown so green it almost glowed, covered with sparkly sequins and cut low in the back for her wings to hang free. She lifted the dress out of the box.

"It's so beautiful," Meghan said, her words coming out in a sigh. "Like something a princess would wear."

"Well, you're my princess." Mimi came around the table and stood behind Meghan, gazing down at the dress. "I've been working on it in the living room for the past few weeks. I hid everything in the back of the hall closet each night—I didn't want you to see it before the sequins were sewn on." She laughed. "That old sewing machine clacks so loud I thought for sure it would wake you up. It's a costume, sweetie, like the one I wear when I perform."

"Thank you!" Meghan said, craning her neck to look up at her mother. "I love it!"

Mimi smiled. "Try it on."

# CHAPTER EIGHTEEN

# Circus Family

MEGHAN STEPPED INTO the gown and zipped up the low back. She twirled into the kitchen. "How do I look?"

"Gorgeous!" Mimi said. "Like a shamrock princess. And it fits you perfectly." She patted the chair beside her. "Sit down for a minute. I have something important to ask you."

Meghan lowered herself onto the chair, careful not to snag the sequins on her dress. Maybe this was about whatever her mom and Grandpa had been discussing that morning when her mom first returned, when she overheard the two of them talking by the roses.

Mimi fiddled with the ribbon from the gift box. She cleared her throat and took a long sip of coffee before looking up to meet Meghan's eyes. "How would you like to come live with me?" she asked, her words running together in a breathless burst.

Meghan's heartbeat thrummed in her ears. "But I already live with you," she said. "And Grandpa."

"I have a very nice home with the circus, sweetie—I'm actually one of the main attractions. The star of the show!" Mimi trilled a little laugh.

"You are? But I thought you were one of the people they shoot out of a cannon."

"I am, and then I fly up to the top of the tent and put on an aerial show. The audience thinks my wings are fake and the flying is just an act." She stood and pulled a pitcher of orange juice out of the refrigerator. "Of course my circus family knows the truth," she added, "but we don't tell outsiders our business."

Meghan felt like she'd been punched in the stomach. *Circus family? I'm her family!*

Grandpa walked in from the garden and glanced at Meghan in her sparkly green dress. "I thought you were making something for yourself," he said, turning to Mimi. He nudged the kitchen faucet on with his elbow and washed his mud-caked hands.

"It's a costume, Dad. It matches one I already have." Mimi wiped the table with a dishcloth and said, "We were talking about Meghan's options…about her future."

Mimi took three glasses out of the cupboard and set them on the table next to the pitcher of orange juice. She and Grandpa looked past each other, not making eye contact. The loudest sound in the kitchen was the ticking of the clock. Grandpa settled into a chair and waited.

Mimi gazed at Meghan and continued. "There are plenty of other children who'd be traveling with us. Most of the older kids perform with their parents. They're a great group—I know you'd make friends right away." She poured more coffee into her cup and sat down next to Meghan. "And there'd be no problem keeping up with your school work—we have a tutor, he's fantastic. The kids do lessons every morning, and practice with their parents in the afternoon." She smiled brightly. "We're all very close, like one big family. Everyone has a great time together!"

Grandpa stood and splashed some coffee into a cup, took a few gulps, and left the cup on the counter. "I'll be in the strawberry patch," he said. "Danged weeds are choking the plants." He walked out the kitchen door.

Meghan's throat ached, a lump made it difficult to swallow. "But what about Brian?" she asked. "I thought maybe you were falling in love with him."

"I'm not in love with him, sweetie. We're just enjoying each other's company."

Meghan reached for the pitcher and poured herself a glass of juice. She glanced at her mother. She didn't want to ruin Brian's surprise, but she had no choice—her mom might not want to leave if she knew what he was planning.

"Remember when you dropped me off at the library to meet Jade and Kayla last week? Well, Brian was there too, but he didn't see us. It looked like he was researching something important…we didn't want to disturb him." *Okay, so maybe we were spying, but it was for a good cause.*

Her mother stared at her, drinking her coffee and waiting for Meghan to get to the point.

"He was checking out romantic cookbooks, and he even got a book about being a step-parent." Meghan paused. *Sorry Brian, I have to tell her.* "I think he's going to ask you to marry him."

Mimi's eyes widened. "What? I like him a lot, and I'm glad you like him too. He's a great guy." She took a sip of her coffee. "We've had a good time together, but I hope he's not planning to propose!"

What about that dreamy expression, the secret smiles? And Brian was handsome, and smart, and kind—like her dad. Didn't that mean anything? *Maybe you just need more time.*

Her mother's voice snapped Meghan back to attention. "It's an amazing feeling to see your name on the marquee, and flying in front of an audience, hearing them clap and cheer—pretty exciting, don't you think?"

Tears prickled behind Meghan's eyes. If only her mom would marry Brian! But Meghan wasn't getting left behind again, not this time. She took a deep breath and swiped her eyes with the backs of her hands.

Mimi sighed. "Imagine how many kids dream about joining the circus and traveling all over the world. It's an incredible opportunity, sweetie. And there's plenty of space in my trailer for the two of us," she added. "You could bring all your things, and you'd have your own phone and laptop to stay in touch with your friends."

Meghan looked up. "Really?"

Her mother smiled. "You can send pictures from Montreal, Paris, London. Who knows—you might meet the Queen of England! There's no telling what doors will open, once we've perfected our act."

She gave Meghan's hand a gentle squeeze. "You'll be a star, sweetie. It's a once in a lifetime chance."

"I guess it would be pretty cool to be a star."

Mimi laughed, the sound tinkling like champagne glasses clinking together.

"But what about Grandpa?"

"Grandpa will stay here at the farm," her mother said. "We can visit him a lot, I promise."

••

THE NEXT MORNING dawned clear and pink, with only a few wispy clouds in the sky.

"Wake up, sweetie." Mimi bent down and gently shook Meghan's shoulders. "There's something I want us to do."

Meghan pulled on a fleece hoodie and jeans, and then stumbled off to brush her teeth.

"Hurry," Mimi called softly, "before the rest of the world wakes up."

She opened the window. "We can go out this way," she said when Meghan returned, "so we don't disturb your grandfather." Cold air flooded into their warm bedroom.

Meghan rubbed her hands together before tucking them into the front pocket of her hoodie. She glanced at her mother. Mimi wore a faded blue sweatshirt with daisies arranged in a peace sign on the front, her honey-brown hair pulled back in a ponytail. With her face freshly scrubbed and not a scrap of makeup, she looked too young to be anyone's mother.

One at a time they sat on the windowsill and flapped hard, lifting off into the crisp morning air. A stiff breeze caught their wings and pushed them over the hills and into town. Soon the streets looked familiar. Up ahead was the little neighborhood park with the swing set and seesaw. Meghan remembered playing there with Jade when they were three or four. Beside it was their old house.

They hovered, winging forward and back in the brisk current, before lowering themselves to the sidewalk.

"Do you remember when I made those?" Mimi pointed to the pink and white checkered curtains still hanging in the upstairs window, Meghan's old room. Her face creased in lines of sorrow. "We were so happy."

Meghan nodded. If she spoke she might start crying. She'd been on this block many times since her dad died, but she never let her eyes linger on the house. She wondered if blue sky and clouds were still painted on the ceiling.

A white house at the end of the block caught Meghan's eye. Two oak trees stood in the front yard, pink flowers lined the window boxes, and a wide wooden swing hung from beams on the front porch. Sparkling dew covered the thick lawn, with a 'For Rent' sign posted in the middle, gleaming in the early morning light.

Meghan's heart leaped. She could almost see her mother and Brian sitting on that front porch swing—talking and laughing, and falling in love. *She just needs more time.*

A neighbor stepped outside and picked up his newspaper. He stopped and stared at them. Mimi lifted her hand in a half-hearted wave before turning away from their old house and flapping into the air.

A breeze funneled through the center of town, sailing them like paper airplanes across the sky. Cars moved about the streets and shops began opening their doors.

A little girl tugged her mother's hand and pointed up at the sky. "Look! It's that butterfly girl and her mom!"

Meghan waved. Butterfly Girl. It sounded nice.

"Oh, I like that!" Mimi said. "Butterfly Girl is perfect! They call me 'Mimi the Magnificent' at Ringman Brothers. I think I'll change that—we'll be 'The Butterfly Lady' and 'The Butterfly Girl.'"

She grinned and began flapping her wings in time with Meghan's. "We'll be an incredible team, a first-class act. Think of all the choices: TV, book deals, movies—we'll be millionaires! For you and me, the sky is the limit!" Mimi's laugh trilled through the air.

Meghan smiled. "A movie would definitely be awesome."

"And you know what?" Mimi added, raising her voice above the wind. "We'll be rich enough to give Grandpa all the money he needs. He can hire workers, buy a fancy new tractor, whatever he wants. He won't have to work so hard, and he can visit us whenever he wants to, without worrying about the farm." She gave Meghan a reassuring smile. "And of course we'll visit him too."

••

THAT NIGHT MEGHAN dreamed of flying at the circus, soaring and twirling high above a screaming crowd. Her mother stood at the center ring, waving a pink and white checkered flag.

Suddenly Meghan jerked awake. Angry voices echoed down the hallway.

"Mary Margaret," Grandpa said, "this here's a good life for a child! She doesn't need fortune and fame, she needs a home."

"How can you say she won't have a home? She'll be with me." Mimi's voice grew shrill. "And you may not realize it, but she's not a child anymore. She's a young woman. She needs her mother."

"She needs her mother? Where have you been? I tried to reach you last summer when her wings first grew—last summer!"

"How can anyone reach you with the phone off the hook!"

"It was before all those yahoos started calling." Grandpa's voice rumbled down the hall like distant thunder. "The phone worked just fine."

"We were in the middle of a ten-city tour, Dad. I didn't get your message until weeks later. You should have told them it was urgent."

"You should have returned my call, Mary Margaret. And how many years have you had a cell phone? Your family shouldn't have to call that godforsaken circus to get a hold of you!" He lowered his voice. "The truth is you were too busy to interrupt your glamorous life."

Meghan slid out of bed, tiptoed along the wall, and stood motionless behind the door. She didn't want to miss a single word.

"I came as soon as I saw her on the news."

Meghan strained to listen. She held her breath.

When her mother finally spoke, Meghan heard tears in her voice. "Dad, you're not being fair. If I had called, she'd ask me why I stayed away. What could I tell her? I couldn't tell her the truth. You know I didn't want to influence her about growing wings."

"I've never understood your thinking on that, seeing as how your own dad has wings." He paused. "For goodness sakes, Mary Margaret, you knew about my wings from the time you were a little bitty baby. You decided for yourself—what makes you think Meghan couldn't figure her own way? She's plenty smart."

"But you wanted her to live here." Mimi paused and blew her nose. "Why are you throwing it back in my face?"

"Well, of course I wanted her to live here. The circus is no place for a child. But you can't go pulling her away from me now. She has a good life here."

"I can give her a good life too! She's growing up, she needs me."

"What she needs is a stable home." Grandpa spoke as if the conversation was over. "You couldn't give it to her then and you can't give it to her now. But you're always welcome to come home. Or visit anytime you like."

A cupboard door slammed. "She's my daughter, Dad. I think I know what's right for her. And when are you going to start calling me Mimi like everyone else?"

Silence stretched into the hallway. Meghan reached for the doorknob to open the door a crack. She listened, her ear to the door, ready to turn the knob.

A chair scraped against the floor.

Meghan froze.

"Mimi suits you," Grandpa said. "It's all about me-me." He barked a short, sharp laugh. "You're the one who wants to be a big shot, and now that sweet girl is getting dragged along with you."

"I'm not dragging her anywhere!" Her mother's voice grew louder. "She wants to go, and why shouldn't she? Who wouldn't want a chance to be a star?"

She paused, and her voice softened. "You're holding her back, Dad. You're holding her back."

Muffled words, and then the sound of the faucet turning on. Grandpa must be filling the kettle for tea. "Promise me you won't push her. Let her make up her own mind."

Cups clanked. Silverware clinked.

Silence.

Someone was coming down the hall!

Meghan tiptoed back to bed and pulled the covers up high. She rolled onto her side and closed her eyes. *Breathe, breathe. Nice and steady. Breathe.*

The door creaked open, and then closed. Was it Grandpa, or her mother? Hard to tell.

# A Birth Night Gift

HER MOTHER'S EYES were puffy the next morning, and Grandpa's had dark bags beneath them. They moved quietly around the kitchen, neither one saying much. Meghan concentrated on eating her toast. Her throat felt tight, and the crumbs scratched when she swallowed.

"I wish you weren't leaving," she said, as she helped carry Mimi's luggage to her car after breakfast. She gazed at her mother's face, trying to lock every detail into her memory.

Mimi hugged her. "Your grandpa and I just need a little break, but I'll be back to get you in a few weeks. Then we'll never be apart again."

Grandpa opened the front door. "Be careful driving," he called out, "and wear your seatbelt, okay?"

"Thanks, Dad," she answered. "I will."

Meghan walked down the driveway and unlatched the gate for Mimi. She waved until her mother's car disappeared between the hills, driving north to her circus home in Seattle. Soon Meghan would be doing the same thing, but how could she leave Grandpa? Her mother simply *had* to fall in love with Brian. If she'd give him more time, and give herself a chance to love again…

*When she comes back, I'll tell her about that house for rent.* But what if her mom still wanted to leave Apple Creek? Meghan would miss Grandpa so much, and Jade and Kayla, too—but she couldn't stay behind again, she just couldn't.

Thinking about her friends reminded her—it was almost time for her birthday.

Meghan jogged up the driveway and onto the front porch. Grandpa had left the front door open. She strode across the living room and into the kitchen, where she found Grandpa drinking coffee and reading a planting almanac.

"Grandpa," Meghan said, "it's almost my birthday."

"It is indeed! Time flies around here." He laughed at his own joke. "What would you like to do for your birthday?" He folded the corner of the page he was reading. "You can invite your friends for a picnic and games. I seem to recall a nice young man…"

"Grandpa!" Meghan's cheeks turned red.

He scratched his chin and furrowed his brow. "Now what was his name? Ah, yes. Now I remember. I believe his name was Danny." He gave her a playful wink.

"Grandpa! Cut it out!"

"All right," he said, "no talking about boys. Who would you like to invite?"

"Just Jade and Kayla. Can we have a sleepover?"

"Sure," he said. "A best-friends-only party."

••

ON THE MORNING of her thirteenth birthday, Meghan walked into the kitchen and found Grandpa elbow-deep in flour, eggs, and cocoa. He turned off the mixer and smiled at her.

"Happy birthday, teenager."

"Finally!" She opened a cupboard and began rummaging around.

"I've got oatmeal on the stove, if you'd like."

"Thanks, I'll have some in a bit." She pulled out granola, pretzels, peanuts, and chocolate chips. "I'm making snacks for when my friends get here."

Jade and Kayla arrived after lunch, dropped off by Kayla's mother.

"I made something special for us," Meghan said, as her friends followed her into the kitchen. She opened the fridge and pulled out a glass pitcher full of tangy, fresh-squeezed lemonade. Beautifully shaped lemon slices and long sprigs of mint floated among the ice cubes.

"Fancy!" Jade said.

Kayla took a sip. "Delish! It tastes as good as it looks."

The girls brought their drinks out to the giant oak tree, where Meghan had spread a bright quilt that morning. A soft breeze carried the fragrance of summer flowers and fresh-mowed grass. The three friends stretched out in the shade and talked about everything. Well, almost everything.

Meghan had put it off long enough—she had to tell them about Mimi's plan. She drew a long, slow breath, willing the words to come out of her mouth. *Just say it.* "My mom wants me to go to Seattle with her. We'd do an act together for the circus."

"That sounds exciting," Kayla said. "How long will you be gone?"

"Well, she wants me to live there, with her, except when we're traveling with the circus. And I guess we might stay in Hollywood for a while, if we do a TV show or a movie."

"Oh…" Jade's mouth dropped open. "I'll miss you so much!" Her lower lip began to tremble.

Meghan sipped her lemonade. She couldn't meet her friend's eyes—if she did they would both start crying. She had grown up with Jade. They'd been friends since they were old enough to talk.

"My mom said she'll buy me a phone and my own laptop for us to stay in touch. And it's not like we'd never see each other in person," Meghan added. "I'll still come back to visit."

Meghan's gaze wandered from the wooden house to the rambling garden. The corn had grown tall, it would be ready to harvest soon. She and Grandpa had planted the tiny kernels, pushing each one gently into the earth. The avocado tree she'd started as a seed had turned into a towering, thick-trunked beauty with glossy leaves, ready to bear fruit, and the fragrant jasmine, once a tiny plant, now ran along the fence and burst with star-shaped flowers. *I'll miss everyone and everything about this place.*

Kayla stared at her hands, twirling a ring on her finger, and blinking fast. "I'm happy for you, being with your mum and in the movies will be amazing—but I wish you didn't have to move away."

"There's still a chance I won't." Jade and Kayla looked up, hopeful. "If my mom falls in love with Brian Richards, I doubt she'll want to leave."

Kayla's eyes widened. "You've got to give him a chance to cook for her! *'Dinner a Deux,'* remember?"

Meghan shook her head. "She told me she's not ready to get married, but if she has more time I'm almost positive she'll fall in love. I've got to convince her to stick around long enough to see how she really feels about him. The problem is she's kind of fed up with my grandfather. They love each other, but they argue about stuff, too."

She turned to Jade. "Did you notice that house for rent at the end of your block? I think my mom would really like it. Then she wouldn't feel so crowded by my grandfather."

"That would be perfect!" Jade rubbed her eyes with the backs of her hands. "We'd be neighbors again."

Grandpa opened the kitchen door and called out, "Are you girls ready for cake?"

"Yes!" Meghan answered, glad to change the subject. She glanced at her friends. "Be right back."

••

"Wow, Grandpa. That's beautiful!" The tall round cake, frosted in green and circled with small purple flowers from the garden, sat in the center of an ancient silver platter. Grandpa stuck the thirteenth candle into the chocolate cake's thick frosting.

He winked at her. "I have a little birthday present for you." He was holding a black book tight under his arm—*The McCoy Family Register.* He beckoned Meghan closer.

Meghan leaned forward to read the faded script. Written on one side of the page was a recipe for Shamrock Cake. The other side had a list of instructions and a poem, or a spell?

Meghan gasped. "Oh my gosh, Grandpa! This is awesome. Do you think it will work?"

Grandpa chuckled. "It's worth a try. But you've got to be sure it wouldn't frighten your friends. Not right to surprise someone with a thing like that if it's not welcome."

"I think they'll love it, but I'll find out for sure."

He smiled and held out the book. Meghan studied the words carefully.

"If you fall asleep you'll miss your chance," Grandpa said. "Timing's pretty clear."

"But a bunch of it's not up to me." She checked the instructions one more time. "What about the moon, and the butterflies?"

He shrugged. "We'll do what we can and hope for the best."

Meghan smiled up at him. "Thanks, Grandpa. I'll hide the book in my pillowcase."

"Don't thank me yet. There's no guarantee about anything except you staying up too late." He grinned. "But I *can* guarantee that this here cake is going to be delicious, if I do say so myself."

Meghan laughed, and then ran to her room to tuck the book out of sight.

They walked outside with the cake and a tray loaded with lemonade, plates, forks, and a wide chef's knife for cutting and serving, and set everything on the table by the roses. Meghan waved to Jade and Kayla. "Time for cake!" she called.

And time to blow out the candles.

# The Shamrock Cake

MEGHAN SUCKED IN a deep breath and closed her eyes. *I wish my friends could fly.* She opened her eyes and blew hard, careful not to miss a single candle. Wisps of smoke curled into the air and floated away.

Jade helped her pull out the burned candles, stopping to lick the frosting off the ends. "Wow!" Jade said. "This is an awesome cake."

Grandpa smiled at her and served each of them a thick wedge.

Sighs of satisfaction rose from around the table. Grandpa was a talented cook, but baking was his forte.

"Mmm, that was so good!" Meghan said, as she scooped the last forkful from her plate. The cake was a rich chocolate with a hint of unusual spice.

"Have another piece, why don't you?" Grandpa said. "It's your birthday. You can have whatever you like."

Meghan rubbed her stomach. "No thanks, I can't fit another bite."

"How about you, Jade? Another piece, Kayla?"

Jade smiled at him but shook her head.

"I can't say no," Kayla said. "But only a sliver, please."

"It's called Shamrock Cake." Grandpa served her a thin slice. "Recipe's been in the family for years. You've had carrot cake? Well, Shamrock Cake has a bit of clover mixed in—gives it extra luck for making birthday wishes come true." He winked at Meghan, then loaded the cake onto the tray and turned toward the house. "You girls enjoy yourselves, now."

The three friends sat at the table, talking and laughing. A group of brown speckled butterflies circled above their heads. Only Meghan noticed as one rested on Kayla's back, and another settled onto Jade's shoulder.

Birds twittered, and a stiff breeze swirled leaves off the ground. Long shadows stretched across the garden.

"We've been outside for hours," Meghan said.

"It's beautiful here." Kayla's gaze swept the garden, now tinged with gold in the afternoon light. "I completely lost track of time."

Jade shivered. "I'm chilly. Let's go inside."

••

Kayla wandered around the cozy living room. "Do you have a computer?" she asked.

"My grandfather keeps it in his bedroom. He does bills and stuff on it. I use it for school, but he's kind of strict about internet." Meghan opened a wooden trunk filled with puzzles and board games. "We can play a game, or maybe watch a movie. We're pretty low tech around here." She shrugged, embarrassed. "Sometimes he doesn't even keep the phone hooked up. We just plug it in when we need to call out. It's like living a hundred years ago."

"I like it," Kayla said. "It's peaceful out here, and your grandfather's great."

"Who says I'm great?" Grandpa walked through the doorway carrying a giant pizza. Kayla smiled.

Meghan grinned up at him. "Thanks, Grandpa. That looks amazing."

"Cheese and veggie pizza, made with zucchini, basil, and tomatoes from the garden, picked fresh this morning." He set it down on the coffee table. "And there's cake in the fridge."

The girls ate pizza, watched a movie, munched on Meghan's pretzel party-mix, and polished off giant slices of cake. The evening flew by.

Jade and Kayla carried their sleeping bags into Meghan's room. She unfolded the futon couch. It was just wide enough to lay their sleeping bags side by side.

"It's almost a full moon," Meghan said. She opened the window. The three friends stared up at the white ball suspended in the sky. Moonlight splashed across the garden, washing the world with a silver glow.

Jade and Kayla climbed into their sleeping bags.

"Do you want to play Truth or Dare?" Meghan asked.

Kayla covered a yawn. "I think I'm too tired."

"We don't have to stay up late," Meghan said. "How about one question? And I promise, however you answer won't hurt my feelings."

Kayla smiled. "Go ahead. Now you've got me too curious to fall asleep."

"Okay, so the question is, would you want wings if you could have them?"

Jade rolled onto her side and propped her head up with her hand. "Who wouldn't want to be able to fly?"

Meghan breathed out a light laugh and said, "Well, a lot of people like the idea of flying, but that doesn't mean they'd actually want to sprout weird appendages." She shrugged, using the tops of her wings instead of her shoulders.

"Why are you asking?" Jade's eyes shined in the moonlight. "Any chance for us to get wings?"

"If it were up to me, I'd give you wings right now." Meghan smiled. "I would love it if all three of us could fly."

"I dream about flying sometimes, when I'm asleep," Jade said.

Kayla sighed. "Flying dreams are wonderful. I never want them to end."

They chatted quietly until the pauses stretched long between sentences and Jade and Kayla's breaths grew slow and deep. Meghan peeked over the side of her bed. They had fallen asleep.

She sat up and leaned against the headboard. The sound of distant crickets droned a steady, soothing rhythm. Time slowly trickled by. Her eyelids drooped, and she started to doze.

*Tick, tick.* She half-heard the clock in the hall double-click before softly chiming midnight. Meghan snapped awake—she'd been waiting for that chime. She eased the family book out of her pillowcase, tilted it into the moonlight so she could see the page, and read the words out loud:

> *"A candle wish I ask of thee,*
> *From earth unfettered, winged and free.*
> *In my stead I ask for friends,*
> *A birth night gift 'til dusk to lend.*
> *Through veins of friendship loyal and true,*
> *Limbs of wonder grow anew.*
> *I call on you, 'tis birthright to ask,*
> *And set loose magic from days gone past.*
> *Grant this boon, no more to lack,*
> *Once I ask, no turning back."*

Meghan tucked the book back into her pillowcase and pulled the covers up to her chin. She smiled to herself and closed her eyes.

••

"Meghan! Meghan, wake up!" Someone kept pushing her shoulder. Meghan blinked her eyes open. Jade was leaning over her, grinning. Sunlight peeked around the edges of the curtains. "I grew wings!"

"Me too!" Kayla said, reaching backward. "They're under my nightgown."

Meghan scrambled out of bed. "I can't wait to see them!" She grabbed two tank tops from her dresser and handed them to her friends.

"Ready?" Meghan said, once the girls had finished changing. "Ta-da!" She pulled the curtains all the way open. Jade and Kayla's golden-brown wings shimmered in the early morning light.

"Look at those green speckles on the edges. They're so shiny!" Meghan clapped her hands. "My birthday wish came true."

"*Your* wish came true? This is my dream come true. I've always wanted to fly." Kayla twirled around to see her reflection in the mirror above Meghan's dresser. "This is absolutely extraordinary!"

"What's going on, Meghan?" Jade asked. "Last night you said you couldn't give us wings. And now..." she flapped her wings to finish making her point.

Kayla's face froze in a strained smile. "No worries if you're a witch—we know you're a good one. We won't tell anyone."

"I'm not a witch!" Meghan's voice squeaked in surprise. "Please don't ask a lot of questions. I don't have any magical powers..." She paused, glancing back and forth between Kayla and Jade. "You could call it 'access' to magic."

"Oh...your grandfather!" Kayla said. "Now I get it."

"That's not—"

"Do you remember dressing up when we were little and pretending we were fairy princesses?" Jade slowly opened and closed her wings. "This is the real deal. I can't even believe it!"

Meghan grinned at her friends. "They're only for the day," she said. "You'll be back to normal by sunset."

Jade fluttered her wings, lifting herself a few inches off the floor. "Let's go flying right now. I don't want to miss a minute."

Grandpa knocked on the door. "Anybody in there ready for breakfast?"

"Come in, Grandpa," Meghan said. "Look what happened!"

Grandpa opened the door. "Well, don't the two of you look grand!" He beamed at Jade and Kayla. "Go ahead and try out your wings. But this is serious, girls. Your wings won't last past sunset. When the sun drops low in the sky, you head for the ground. Don't take any chances." Meghan remembered the words, but she didn't say them out loud. *A birth night gift 'til dusk to lend.*

The lines on Grandpa's forehead wrinkled deeper. "Best if you keep your flying right here on our property, and not too high."

"I'll make sure we stay safe," Meghan said. "We might want to explore a bit, but I promise we'll be careful." She turned to her friends, who looked as if they might fly from pure excitement alone. "Let's go outside so you can see how they feel."

With a few strong pushes, Meghan flew above the rooftop and turned graceful circles in the air. Jade and Kayla flapped hard and lifted off, and then quickly landed. Meghan hovered nearby. "Don't worry," she said. "Your survival instinct will take over—you won't fall or crash into anything, unless you're not paying attention to where you're going." They tried again, this time soaring above the house before fluttering back down to the grass.

"Sweet!" Jade said. "All you have to do is flutter to slow down." Soon the three friends were racing above the garden. Happy shrieks and shouts filled the air.

The kitchen door swung open. "Time for breakfast!" Grandpa called, waving them down from the sky.

The three girls followed him into the house. "Mmm, pancakes, my favorite," Meghan said. She opened the fridge. "I'll get us some milk." Jade and Kayla settled in at the table.

"Fuel up, girls." Grandpa slid a stack of pancakes onto each plate. "Flying feels easy, but there's muscles at work you never knew you had."

"Not to mention some you never had," Meghan added.

"No problem," Jade said. "I'm starving!"

"Me too." Kayla drizzled syrup on her pancakes. "This looks fantastic."

"Now, keep your flying to where there's no other people," Grandpa said, jerking his thumb toward the part of the forest where the mountains rose above the tree line. "And keep your eyes open—there's no public walking trails on this side of the mountain, too steep and rocky, but hikers and campers still come around here once in a while. Whatever you do, don't let anyone take your picture. We'd have those blasted reporters swarming all over us again, asking questions." He glanced at Meghan. "There's more to the McCoy wings than simple genetics…things we can't talk about."

He gave Jade and Kayla a long look. "Remember, first sign of sunset you *land*." The lines in his forehead creased deeper. "And stay out of sight—no photographs. The consequences are very high."

Jade and Kayla answered him with a solemn nod.

"I need to do a few things in town, but you girls help yourselves to whatever you want." He lifted his hand in a quick goodbye. Soon the sound of his truck's old engine filled the air.

"What is he?" Kayla asked. "Some kind of wizard, or a warlock?"

Meghan laughed. "He's not a wizard, and definitely not a warlock! He would never do any kind of witchcraft. He just knows a lot of ancient stuff."

Jade nodded and said, "I always suspected he was a wizard. He has that wise old soul thing about him."

"Jade, you've known him forever. Did you ever see him doing wizard things?"

"What do you call these?" Jade flapped her wings to make her point. "And what was all that about 'consequences,' like something terrible will happen if anyone takes our picture?"

"He was talking about reporters snooping around and pestering us all the time, and you too if you got your picture taken." She shrugged. "And how can he explain how your wings grew when you're not McCoys?"

Kayla shook her head. "Meghan, the more you tell us he's not a wizard, the more certain we are that he is. But no worries, you don't have to explain. It's all right—it's wonderful, actually. You're very lucky."

••

Meghan filled a satchel with snacks and bottles of water, along with shirts to cover their wings, just in case. "I know a beautiful place where we can hang out. It's hidden, hard to find unless you know where to go, and there's no way for anyone else to get there unless they're rock climbers. And anyway, we'd see them before they spotted us."

They soared over the forest behind the house and caught the thermal updraft that curved up the side of the mountain. Meghan led the way to the waterfall where she and her mother had spent so much time earlier that summer. The girls hovered mid-air and let the cool spray mist their hot skin before wading barefoot along the edges of the rocky pool, collecting colorful stones worn smooth by the tumbling water. The morning flew by.

"So, what do you want to do next?" Meghan asked. She opened her satchel and handed out apples and granola bars. "We can look for thimble berries. I picked some last week—they're in season right now."

"We can do that anytime, hiking," Jade said. "I want to show my mom." She grinned and bit into her apple, wiggling her wings up and down as she chewed.

Meghan laughed, but shook her head. "She wouldn't tell anyone, but that little park is right there, and neighbors. Someone for sure would take your picture."

"Your grandfather is very kind," Kayla said, "but I wouldn't dare go against his orders." Her eyes widened. "Imagine getting zapped with a pair of frog legs or a tail full of turkey feathers." She tore the wrapper off her granola bar and took a bite.

Meghan rolled her eyes. "Think what you want, but he's not a wizard."

"Í know!" Jade said. "Let's see who's hanging out at the soccer field. There's usually a few kids from school, but we can warn them not to take our picture." Meghan perked up. Maybe Danny would be there—she hadn't seen him since the party on the last day of school.

The girls finished eating and stuck their empty wrappers back in the satchel. They pushed off and flapped forward until a strong updraft lifted them higher, leveling out a thousand feet above the forest.

"Follow me," Meghan called, as she switched directions. Suddenly she jetted ahead, her hair streaming straight behind her. Jade and Kayla caught up, whooping and laughing, all three of them coasting on the powerful crosscurrent that flowed above the hills that led into town.

"Flying feels so natural," Kayla said, "like I've been doing it all my life!"

Meghan smiled at her friend. "It's like swimming on the wind. Easy once you get the hang of it."

The girls gradually descended to a lower altitude. They'd be easier to spot now. Meghan scanned the edge of town in the distance, making sure the few cars on the road weren't slowing down or pulling over to take a picture. An old man ambled along the sidewalk with two little dogs on leashes, and a group of teenagers streaked past him on bikes, but they never looked up.

Nope. No pictures to worry about.

The three girls swooped over the last hill. Danny's friends were playing football at the soccer field. Greta's girls sat in the grass on the sideline, tanning their legs and watching the boys.

"Let's keep the school between us and the soccer field," Meghan said, "then head for the tree." She pointed to the huge chestnut tree that grew near the edge of the field. "We can check things out and decide if we want to stay."

No one noticed as Meghan, Jade, and Kayla glided behind the building and fluttered to the ground. They pressed silently along the side of their school until they had a clear view of the soccer field.

Someone punted the ball. Both teams started running.

Greta's girls turned their heads to watch the boys.

"Hurry!" Meghan said, pushing off for the tree.

Jade touched down a few seconds behind her. She wrapped her legs around the thick branch and held onto one beside her, steadying herself. "I wonder where

Danny is," Jade said, peeking at the field through a gap in the leaves.

Kayla had landed on a limb below the other two girls. She stood and held onto Jade's branch. "At least Greta's not here," she said.

Meghan searched the field. Her heart sank. "They're probably off doing something, together."

Kayla shook her head. "No way. He's far too nice. He wouldn't hang out with her unless he couldn't avoid her, like at school, or the fair."

Jade glanced over her shoulder and sucked in a sharp breath. "Uh…is that who I think it is?"

# CHAPTER TWENTY-ONE

# Danny and Greta

DANNY AND GRETA coasted into sight on Danny's bike. Greta perched on the seat and held onto Danny's waist, her long legs extended out to the sides. Danny pedaled standing up. He was breathing hard as they swung around the corner of the school.

He leaned his bike against the trunk of the chestnut tree. Meghan and her friends peered down through the leafy branches.

Greta smiled at him. "Thanks for the ride."

"Always glad to help a damsel in distress," he replied, bowing low and doffing an imaginary hat. Greta's flirty giggle was interrupted by one of Danny's friends calling out and throwing him a long pass. Danny scrambled to catch it, and Greta sauntered off to join her friends.

"Do you want to leave?" Jade asked, noticing Meghan's pale, stony face. "We don't have to hang out here."

"No, we can stay. I figured they'd get together over the summer. It's no big deal." If only he wasn't so nice, and smart. And cute.

The girls pushed off the tree and glided down to the grass.

"Look who's here," Greta said. "It's our favorite celebrity, and her groupies sprouted wings too. Must be contagious."

Nikki snickered. She glanced at Meghan. "Sorry, I couldn't resist. But how did Jade and Kayla get wings?"

"I'm not really allowed to talk about it," Meghan answered.

A dark-haired girl gazed wide-eyed at Meghan and her two friends. Meghan recognized her, she was Nikki's little sister, soon to be a sixth grader. "Can you give me wings too?" she asked Meghan, smiling shyly.

Greta stared at her. "Why would you even go there? If you want to fly, learn how to hang glide. It's a lot better than having weird flappy things dangling off you." She wrinkled her nose. "What a freak-fest."

Jade's eyes flashed. "Jealous much?"

Meghan did her best to smile at the younger girl. "Sorry, it's not up to me."

"Don't you have to help your grandfather or something?" Greta asked.

Meghan's heart pounded, but her voice came out smooth. "But Greta, what about that little chat we had?

You said you wanted us to spend more time together, maybe even hang out with your group at lunch next year."

Greta snorted and glanced at her friends. "Yeah, right. Like that would ever happen." She turned back to Meghan. "Take a hint. No one invited you."

Jade shook her head in disgust. "What is your problem? Get over yourself! And anyway, this is our school too."

Kayla nodded. "We have every right to be here."

"Meghan!" Danny lobbed the football to a friend and jogged toward the girls. He stopped a few feet in front of Meghan, smiling.

"Hi Danny." Meghan's voice shook a little. Her gaze flickered to Jade and Kayla. "Let's go back to the waterfall," she said. "It's cooler there, anyway."

"But you just got here." Danny caught hold of her wrist. "I've been hoping I'd see you."

He tugged her away from the group of girls, steering her gently across the field. "What's the deal with Jade and Kayla's wings?" he asked.

Meghan took a deep breath, hoping it would calm the tremor in her voice. "My grandfather doesn't want me to talk about it. But they'll both be back to normal by the end of the day."

"Too bad," Danny said. "If I had wings I'd want to keep them forever." He glanced over his shoulder at Jade and Kayla. "Totally amazing! Your grandfather is so cool."

Meghan didn't say anything. She didn't want to lie, and she couldn't tell the truth.

Danny let go of her wrist and pushed the shaggy hair out of his eyes. "Why were you leaving so fast?"

"We're not welcome," she said, lifting her chin toward Greta and her girls. "I thought we were starting to get along better, but I guess not."

"Don't worry about her. She's a snob, but she's harmless." He searched Meghan's eyes. "I haven't seen you all summer. I've been trying to call you, but your phone always has a busy signal."

He'd been trying to call her? Heat flushed her cheeks, but she held her gaze steady. "My grandfather keeps the phone unplugged. We get a lot of calls from reporters, and other people pestering us."

She skimmed her foot back and forth across the grass, avoiding his eyes. But she had to know, one way or the other. "Why were you calling me? I thought you liked Greta."

"What? Who told you that?"

She took a deep breath. "No one did. But you hang out with her after school, and give her rides on your bike…"

"I passed her on the way to the field. She wanted a ride, that's all."

Meghan glanced up at him. "It seems like you're always together." She bit the edge of her lip. *Just say it.* "Everyone knows she's crushing on you big time. I figured it was mutual."

Danny's eyebrows flew up. "No way! We're like brother and sister—she just likes to joke around. I've known her since we were little kids."

He shielded his eyes with his hand and looked across the field. Jade and Kayla hovered in the air about fifteen feet above the thirty-yard line. When one of the boys passed the football, Jade snatched it mid-air and tossed it higher. Kayla clutched at it, almost fumbled but managed to hold on, and then swooped over the end zone, gripping the ball in one hand like a trophy. The boys laughed and high-fived each other, cheering Jade and Kayla, who were now whooping loudly and flying victory loops above their heads.

Greta paced back and forth on the sideline, oblivious to the game, shielding her eyes from the sun and talking non-stop to her friend Nikki—but sneaking looks in Meghan and Danny's direction every few seconds. Danny watched her for a moment before turning away.

"My friends say she has a thing for me," he said. "I guess maybe she does."

*Great. Now I've clued him in.*

Danny stared at his feet, shifting his weight from side to side. He glanced at Meghan, and then back at his feet. "It's not Greta that I like," he said quietly.

Red crept up his neck and onto his cheeks. "Would it be all right if I call you? Maybe we could go to the fair together. I think it starts next week."

Meghan's heart pounded so loud she was afraid he might hear it. She took a deep breath, but the air seemed thin and insubstantial, like there wasn't enough oxygen.

She stared at him and filled her lungs again, clearing her head. "I'll make sure the phone is plugged in." Once she started smiling, she couldn't stop. It looked like Danny was having the same problem.

Greta hooked arms with Nikki and strolled across the field. "What are you two doing out there in Siberia?" she called. She walked up to Meghan and Danny, beaming a fake smile. "Who wants to play freeze tag?"

"No thanks," Meghan said. "I have to take off."

Danny laughed. "That's funny!"

"I don't get it," Greta said. "But *too bad* she has to go."

The sarcasm went right past Danny. "Take off," he said. "You know, like fly."

It was hard not to laugh at the war taking place on Greta's face. She needn't have bothered—Danny didn't seem to notice the phony smile that won the battle.

"I'll call you." He reached out and touched Meghan's arm. "Uh, as long as your phone is plugged in." They both laughed.

Meghan waved to Jade and Kayla and called out, "Are you ready to go?" Jade and Kayla smiled down at the boys beneath them, waved, and flapped toward Meghan.

One of the boys shouted, "Kayla! Wait a second—let me get a picture."

Nikki grinned and pulled out her phone. "We can sell them to the newspaper," she said, her voice carrying on the breeze. "Or even better, one of those celebrity gossip magazines—I'm talking *big* bucks."

"No! Don't do it!" Kayla circled back and fluttered to the ground. Meghan and Jade landed nearby. "Her grandfather said absolutely no pictures."

"You do *not* want to mess with him," Jade added.

"He's not going to know." Nikki aimed her phone at Jade and Kayla. "Not unless you tell him."

Before Nikki could click a second shot, Jade leaped forward and twirled in a graceful roundhouse, kicking the phone out of her hand. Nikki stumbled backward and fell on the ground.

"Ow! What did you do that for? And you got my new shorts all dirty!"

Kayla reached out her hand. "She's trying to save your life, you ungrateful little twit." She pulled Nikki up. "Her grandfather will give you green toad skin or grow horns on your head. He can do it if he wants to. He's a very powerful wizard."

"Oh, wow." Nikki lunged for her phone. She clicked it on and scrolled through. "Deleted," she said, shooting a worried glance at Meghan. "Sorry, I didn't know."

"That's okay," Meghan said. "Like you said, you didn't know." Her gaze lingered on each face in the group. "If anyone else has taken pictures, now would be a good time to delete them."

One of Danny's friends took out his cell phone, then one of the girls. "Sorry, Meghan," the girl said, her eyes wide. The boy glanced up from his phone. "Yeah, tell your grandfather we're really sorry. I swear—I deleted everything."

Meghan nodded at them, accepting their apologies. She almost wanted to laugh at how scared they looked, but she had to let them believe it. *This wizard thing is working out nicely.*

# The Ancient Bell

"**N**ATURE'S AIR CONDITIONING is amazing!" Jade said, hovering near Meghan and Kayla in the waterfall's spray. The three friends cooled off, and then played flutter tag, and treetop hide-and-seek. Their laughter rang through the air until—

"Look at the sky!" Meghan pointed to the golden-pink clouds. She grabbed her satchel. "There's a current that flows over the mountain top. It's high—higher than we've been flying today, but it runs right over my grandpa's property."

Jade pressed her lips together in a grim smile. "As long as the sun doesn't go down, right Kayla?"

The color drained from Kayla's cheeks, but she nodded. "We'll keep a close watch."

Jade and Kayla flapped into the air, following Meghan.

A few minutes later, Meghan called out, "I found the current!" Jade and Kayla pushed hard to catch up.

Meghan shouted to be heard over the rush of the wind. "My mom and I fly this route all the time. It's much easier in this direction." She smiled. "Like floating downstream instead of swimming against the current."

"Oh, this is lovely!" Kayla said, keeping her wings stretched open to glide on the stream of air.

Soon the forest spread out below them, and beyond it, the old wooden house.

"I wish my wings would cool down," Kayla said. "They feel quite hot."

"Mine are too, now that you mention it." Jade flapped a few times, and then glided.

Meghan tried to keep her voice calm. "Uh, the wind up here is pretty icy. This isn't a warm thermal—my wing tips are practically frozen." She studied Jade and Kayla's wings as they flew. Nothing seemed wrong, but something must be happening. "I think we're running out of time."

Kayla's eyes grew wide. "Let's land right now!"

Jade shook her head. "We still have time—look where the sun is. It's probably pitch black in the forest at night, and we're still at least a mile away from Meghan's house."

Meghan nodded. "We don't want to get lost in there. We could end up walking around in circles for hours."

The three girls flapped as fast as they could. Jade and Kayla grimaced with effort, racing the setting sun, now a glowing golden ball dangling above the horizon. With a final push, they soared high above the sunflowers by Grandpa's fence.

Meghan glanced over her shoulder. Shadows creased the mountainside, and the clouds had darkened from pink to smoky orange. When she turned back around, something was different. A sliver of the sun's edge had dipped out of sight.

"Get down to the ground!" Meghan cried, her heartbeat thundering in her ears.

Jade and Kayla dove head first for the grass near the old oak tree, their wings fluttering wildly.

"Slow down!" Meghan shouted. "You're going too fast!"

"Tuck and roll!" Jade yelled, ducking her head low against her chest. "Put your head down and get ready to roll!" After years of martial arts, she knew how to fall safely.

Both girls landed on outstretched hands before tumbling forward in a somersault. Meghan touched down behind them.

Jade stood and brushed the leaves off her clothes. "We made it!" she said, grinning at Meghan.

They both turned and looked at Kayla, who was wheezing quietly, staring straight up. "Are you hurt?" Meghan asked.

"She must have got the wind knocked out of her," Jade said, kneeling beside Kayla. "Try to relax, okay?" She glanced up at Meghan. "It happened to me once. Kayla probably flipped hard onto her back." She patted Kayla's arm. "Take some deep, easy breaths."

Kayla gave her a weak smile. "I think I'm all right now," she said, gasping. Jade and Meghan helped her stand.

The three girls began slowly walking toward the house as the sun shot its last rays across the garden, bathing the earth in golden light.

"Something's wrong!" Jade said, tugging on Meghan's arm. Jade and Kayla's wings began to glow, and a strange humming vibrated through the air.

The hum began pulsing like a heartbeat, louder and higher as the seconds ticked by, already so loud they could hardly stand it.

Kayla screamed, "What's happening to us?" Jade and Kayla struggled to move, but they could barely turn their heads or shuffle their feet. As the humming increased, their movements decreased. The sound waves seemed to press against them, locking them in place.

Meghan shouted, "I'll find my grandpa! He'll know what—"

*DONG!* The deep bronze sound of an ancient bell interrupted her, splitting through the humming. Light radiated from Jade and Kayla's wings.

*DING!* The hum was now a silver crystal sound, solemn and lovely, pulsing in the air like church bells.

*DONG! DING! DONG!* Each chime layered over the one before, blending in perfect harmony. The three friends stood awestruck, no longer afraid. The sound was too beautiful to be afraid.

*DINGGG!* A final chime vibrated through the air. Sparkling lights swirled around Jade and Kayla's wings, like twirling diamonds casting rainbow prisms of light. A burst of golden light flashed, and then a blinding blast of green.

Meghan and her friends blinked, still seeing spots from the first flash.

A glittering mist fell around Jade and Kayla's shoulders, like feather-light snow.

Their wings were gone.

The humming stopped. Only the sound of rustling leaves disturbed the quiet. Jade and Kayla hugged their shoulders where their wings had been.

"Are you okay?" Meghan asked.

"My shoulders are killing me," Jade said, "but that was awesome!"

"You're right on time," Grandpa called. He walked across the grass to meet them. "I was watching for you, cut it pretty close—but you made it. That was quite a grand finale. The colors were beautiful." He grinned at Jade and Kayla. "How was the flying?"

"It was amazing!" Jade said, still rubbing her shoulders.

"Fantastic!" Kayla smiled, then winced. "But I feel like I rowed a boat all day. Even my stomach muscles hurt."

"When you're flying fast, you've got to arch your back and keep your legs stretched out," Grandpa said. "It's not something most folks are accustomed to doing."

"I don't mind," Jade said. "Thank you for giving us wings."

Kayla nodded. "Yes! Thanks so much!"

Grandpa smiled and glanced at Meghan. "Just call it a birthday wish come true."

The sun's golden afterglow faded into twilight blue. Grandpa and the girls stood quietly soaking in the last of the day.

The sound of a motor thrummed through the stillness. In the distance, a car inched up the hill and around the bend below the gate. Tires soon crunched along the gravel driveway, kicking up a cloud of summer dust.

Grandpa hurried up the path to meet Kayla's mother, stopping to pick up a cardboard box he'd set on the ground.

The three friends trailed behind. Kayla sighed. "I don't want this day to end."

"We're not saying goodbye today," Meghan said. "I promise we'll see each other again before I leave. That's if we even go—I haven't had a chance to ask my mom about renting that house in our old neighborhood."

"Your mom better say Yes." Jade squeezed her eyes closed for a moment.

Meghan nodded. "I'm pretty sure she'll at least give it a try, especially when I tell her how much I want us to stay here. And before long she'll be so in love with Brian that she'll never want to leave." Meghan wrapped her arm around Jade's shoulders as they headed for the house.

Kayla's mother waved. She stood by her car with Grandpa, chatting.

"We have to get our things!" Kayla called. Her mother was giving Jade a ride home on their way across town.

The three girls shuffled down the hall to Meghan's room. Kayla leaned over and picked up her sleeping bag, then dropped it with a groan and grabbed her shoulder. "Here, let me get them for you." Meghan carried both sleeping bags to the car while Jade and Kayla massaged their sore shoulders.

Grandpa winked at the two girls and said, "They'll probably ache for a day or two." Jade and Kayla shared a grin.

Kayla's mother looked confused until Grandpa handed her the cardboard box he'd been carrying, filled with corn and summer squash. "Oh, thank you! These are absolutely gorgeous," she said. "And I'm so glad the girls got some fresh air and exercise," she added. "Gardening can be a great workout."

Grandpa smiled, but he didn't say anything.

Meghan waved until their car curved down the hill and out of sight. "Thanks, Grandpa," she said, reaching out to hug him. "My friends had a great time. Flying with them was the best birthday present ever."

Grandpa held her close. "You're welcome, darlin'," he said, his words muffling in her hair. He kissed the top of her head. "I would give you the moon and the stars," he whispered, in a voice only he could hear.

••

LATER THAT WEEK, Meghan asked, "Are you sure the phone is plugged in?"

"And good morning to you." Grandpa gave her a long look.

"Sorry, Grandpa. Good morning." She picked up the telephone receiver. The dial tone droned in her ear.

Grandpa leaned back in his chair and blew into his coffee cup. "Go ahead and phone your mother, darlin'. I know you need to get your plans arranged." He sipped his coffee. "Now, my guess is…"

It had only been three days since she flew to the soccer field with Jade and Kayla, but each day seemed longer than the one before. The way Danny smiled, the way he looked at her? Just thinking about it made her heart beat faster. And she hadn't told him that she might be leaving.

"What?" Meghan realized her grandpa was still talking and she hadn't heard a single word he'd said.

"I was saying that your mother is likely to show up any day now."

"That's okay. I'm not in a rush."

But time hurried along on its own, and at four-fifteen the very next day, Meghan heard the sound of Mimi's car crunching the gravel in the driveway.

# Fly Away Home

"THERE'S MY STAR!" Mimi flung open the car door and beamed at Meghan. "I missed you so much."

Meghan gave her mom a hug. "Can I carry anything?" she asked.

"No, I've got it." Mimi grabbed a small leather suitcase from the trunk. "I'm only staying the night. Tomorrow we'll drive to circus headquarters in Seattle. We'll practice our routine for a few weeks and then head on to Vancouver." Her mother was talking very fast. "Canada hardly seems like a foreign country, but we'll need to get you a passport."

Grandpa opened the front door. "Hi Dad," she said, and kissed him on the cheek.

It had been a short walk from the car, but Mimi was breathless. She followed Grandpa to the kitchen, dropped her bag on the floor, and pulled out a chair. The wooden legs scraped across the floor like nails on a chalkboard. Meghan winced.

"How was your drive?" Grandpa asked, leaning against the counter.

"Fine, Dad. Not too much traffic." Mimi's gaze ping-ponged around the room. "It only took four hours." She prattled on, still breathless, chit-chatting about the weather and the condition of the road. The kitchen felt oddly cold, yet stuffy at the same time.

"How long are you staying, Mimi?" Her mother's name sounded awkward when Grandpa said it.

"Just the night. We've got a lot to fit in before Meghan's first performance."

"But what about Brian?" Meghan asked. "Aren't you going to see him while you're in town?"

"No…" her mother paused and looked back and forth between Meghan and Grandpa. "I'm just here to pick you up. And see your grandpa."

"But Mom, Brian is falling in love with you. He's going to ask you to marry him."

Mimi frowned, and then ran a hand over her forehead as if to smooth away the lines. "Sweetie, your dad and I were friends long before we got married—we met in second grade. And when he was twelve or thirteen, he started working here at the farm during the melon harvest each summer. Brian might be thinking about marriage, but it's way too soon."

"It might be too soon right now," Meghan said, "but what if you gave it more time?"

Her mother opened her mouth to speak, but Grandpa held up a hand. "Why not hear her out?" He pulled up a chair and sat down at the table.

"Yeah, Mom. I have a plan." Meghan was ready, she'd thought it all the way through. "There's a really nice house in town—in our old neighborhood. It's for rent. We'd have our own rooms, and I could still see Grandpa every day after school." Her words streamed out, calm and clear. "You could perform with the circus whenever it's in the area, so you'd still see all your friends there. And maybe Grandpa wouldn't mind too much if we did a movie or TV show—right Grandpa?" She glanced at him. "We'd make sure it was quality, not some trashy show."

"We could talk about it." Grandpa turned to her mother. "Why not think about it, sweetheart?"

Mimi pressed her fingers to her temples and held them there for a moment. "Dad, I can't believe you're encouraging this. It's like a fairy tale the two of you have dreamed up where Brian is my prince and we all live happily ever after."

"It's not a fairy tale. It's a possibility." Grandpa put both hands on the table and leaned forward. "Maybe slow down a little," he said. "See where this road takes you. You could move into town and find out what happens, with or without Brian. It's a good life here. And I'm not so stubborn that I can't see my way to watching the two of you flying on TV or in the movies. I think I'd be mighty proud of my butterfly girls."

"Thanks, Dad." Mimi's face was pale and hard. "I love you both and I appreciate what you're trying to do, but let's stop it here."

Grandpa's shoulders drooped. He pushed back his chair and moved to the sink to fill the kettle.

"You'll understand this better when you're older," Mimi said, picking at a loose thread on her blouse. "Falling in love is wonderful, but it isn't enough." She twirled the thread around her finger and snapped it off.

"It wouldn't be fair to Brian either," she added, looking up to meet Meghan's eyes. "He wants a quiet life here in Apple Creek—it's a perfectly good life, but it's not for me." Mimi sighed, shaking her head. "I can't make myself fit into his world. I'd wither up inside."

Her eyes softened in a gentle smile. "You've never experienced it yet, but I promise you, performing for a crowd is incredible! The lights, the costumes…all those people applauding and cheering. It's the most wonderful feeling in the world."

"Better than falling in love?"

"It's different, sweetie. It's loving what you do. They're totally different. What makes me happy is traveling around the world and seeing new sights, meeting new people everywhere I go." Her face lit up. "And you. Being with you again makes me so happy. We're going to have a wonderful life together, I promise."

A lump of disappointment swelled in Meghan's throat. It was such a great plan! If only her mother could be happy here.

*Well that's it, then. We're leaving tomorrow.* The kitchen felt chilly and it got into her stomach. *I need to call Jade and Kayla.* But she didn't move.

"You two go on out, the weather's fine," Grandpa said. "I'll bring us tea when it's ready." Meghan rose stiffly and walked out the kitchen door, shaking her head as if she was clearing away a bad dream.

"Next year Ringman Brothers is touring Europe," her mother said, following Meghan down the long garden path to the table by the roses. "Won't that be exciting!"

Mother and daughter settled into the chairs, turning them so the sun wouldn't shine in their eyes.

Mimi sighed. "This is perfect. I love days like today."

"Me too," Meghan said, leaning back in her chair. She inhaled the blue-sky air, puffs of cotton candy clouds floated in the distance. She looked around the sprawling garden. A new patch of dahlias bloomed in shades of orange and red, she'd have to remember to pick some for the vase in the living room. Her gaze lingered for a moment on the pots of marigolds by the kitchen door, and the fragrant jasmine winding along the fence. She'd planted so many flowers here…

"Do you need help packing?" her mother asked. "We'll be back for Thanksgiving, Christmas at the latest. You don't need to bring much, mostly winter clothes and a decent coat. We can take another load later."

She'd spent so many hours here in this garden. She'd had her thirteenth birthday here. Meghan's gaze rested at the old weathered bench, its slats worn smooth from the hours she and Grandpa sat reading or talking in the shade of the giant oak tree.

"I'm still kind of making up my mind," Meghan said.

Mimi gasped.

Where did that come from? Meghan's own words surprised her, bubbling up from some hidden place inside. "It's not that I don't want to live with you," she said, glancing at Mimi's stricken face, "and I know it's a once in a lifetime opportunity…"

"Have I rushed you?" her mother asked. "You probably want to spend some time with your friends before we go. We don't have to leave tomorrow."

"It's not that." She couldn't look at Mimi's face. "I thought I was sure, but I guess I'm still thinking about it." They sat in silence, staring out at the garden.

The butterflies were out in full force, careening after each other, pure joy and light on wings. They were happy to explore the same roses, play the same butterfly games again and again. They didn't fly far and wide to find new gardens. They stayed here in Grandpa's garden. They were happy here.

Like a sunbeam breaking apart the shadows, Meghan knew. There was no turning back now, she had to say it. She took a deep breath. "Mom…" Meghan willed herself to get the rest of the words out. "I can't go with you. This is where I belong."

She met her mother's eyes, forced herself not to look away. "I don't want to be part of a circus family. Grandpa is my family, and you are too. And that tutor for the circus kids sounds great, but I want to keep going to school with my friends."

How could she hurt her mother like this? But she had to say everything, leave nothing out. "I don't really want to be a star, Mom. I'm happy the way I am—a normal girl who happens to have wings."

Her mother's eyes widened, and then welled with tears. "It's okay, sweetie." She took a deep, ragged breath. "No kid should have to make a decision like this. You and your grandpa can come visit me, and I'll visit you."

A lump of sorrow grew in Meghan's throat, the coppery taste of grief filled her mouth. She was losing her mother, again. "I wish we could just rent a house in town! And I still don't understand—I thought you *wanted* me to be a normal girl. You protected me from seeing your wings, and now I'm supposed to join the circus and go on TV? It doesn't make sense."

Mimi stiffened. She glanced at Meghan, then turned away.

In that one tiny moment, that one unguarded look, Meghan knew the truth. Like a memory pushed way down deep, a kind of 'knowing' shot straight to the surface.

"You wanted to leave! It wasn't about protecting me, you *wanted* to leave."

Mimi flinched. "It's complicated, Meghan."

"Please, Mom—just tell me what happened. Tell me why you left me." Meghan clasped her hands tight in her lap.

Her mother's shoulders sagged. "I love you," she said quietly. "I hope you know that."

Mimi sat with her eyes closed, her fingertips pressing against her eyelids. She rocked back and forth as if comforting herself. "Protecting you wasn't just an excuse," she whispered hoarsely.

After a few minutes, she cleared her throat and sat up straight. "When I was younger," she said, blinking at Meghan, "the last thing I wanted was to be different! I thought you'd feel the same way, and it would be wrong to burden you with such an odd childhood. I knew you could grow wings later, if you wanted to, but I never expected you to want them so soon."

"I'm not you, Mom," Meghan said. "But go on."

"I never meant to be away so long." Mimi wiped her eyes with the backs of her hands. "Only I'm not the kind of person who can stay in one place and live a quiet little life. Your dad knew that about me. We were always planning trips, redecorating the house—he kept me busy so I wouldn't get bored."

She breathed out a long sigh. "I tried to be like my friends. It seemed so important to fit in! When I was a senior in high school I got a job in town like the other girls. We all had boyfriends. I had your dad—over time our friendship had turned into love." She smiled, a faraway look in her eyes. "I was crazy about him, but even then, I felt restless. I wanted to work on a cruise ship and travel, see the world. But your dad wanted to be a firefighter…"

Meghan watched a red-tailed hawk circling in the sky, scanning the ground for an unsuspecting mouse. She couldn't look at her mother.

"Once I got my wings I figured it was my turn, time to have some adventures—become the person I was meant to be." She searched Meghan's face. "Do you understand? It wasn't about you, sweetie. I always loved you. But this," she swept her hand toward the garden and the town below the hills, "this life isn't enough for me, it never was. You want me to be happy, don't you?"

Meghan's stomach squeezed tight. She took a deep breath and unclasped her hands.

A ladybug landed on her finger. Meghan examined its smooth jewel-like back, its glossy black dots shining in the sun.

*Ladybug, ladybug, fly away home. Your house is on fire, your children are alone.*

# CHAPTER TWENTY-FOUR

# Home at Last

MEGHAN WATCHED THE ladybug inch along her finger.

"But now you can come with me," her mother said. "It would make me so happy. And we'd still see your grandpa—often, I promise."

Meghan lifted her hand to her face and blew. The ladybug flew away, high into the end of summer sky. She followed it with her eyes until it faded from sight.

Meghan sighed. "What about my happiness?"

Mimi leaned back, watching her face.

Meghan turned to look at her mother. "You love the circus, traveling from one city to the next, all those people staring at you. But I'm not you. I love this place. I have Grandpa, our garden, my friends…I want to be with you, but I don't want your life."

They were both quiet while Mimi leaned over, pressing the hem of her shirt against her eyes again and again, like they wouldn't stop leaking.

"I am so, so sorry," she said, finally sitting up. She gazed at Meghan. "I haven't been a very good mother."

"Part of it was my fault." Meghan's throat squeezed tight. She swallowed a few times before continuing. "I wish I had told you a long time ago—when Jade and I were little, we played a game called Fairy Princess. We always played it at Jade's house, I guess that's why I never talked about it." She swallowed again, making a strange gulping sound like the words were stuck deep in her throat. "In our game, we pretended we could fly."

She stared at the ground and kicked at a clump of grass. "I already wanted wings—you could have shown me yours right when they first grew. It wouldn't have mattered."

She sighed, glancing up to meet her mother's eyes. "I know the mountains aren't as exciting as the circus, but you probably would have been happy right here, as long as you weren't worried about me finding out about your wings."

"What? Oh sweetie, none of that would have changed anything." Mimi looked out past the hills to where the highway melted into the horizon. "Flying around in the mountains was exciting when my wings first grew, but forever? No. The circus has been a great adventure, a perfect fit for me. But it was no life for a six-year-old girl, moving from town to town."

She paused and pressed her lips together, like she was searching for the right words. "It was a hard choice, sweetie. I wanted us to be together, but I knew you'd be better off here with your grandpa."

Meghan's heartbeat clanged in her ears. "Well, thanks for asking me what I needed! I lost Dad, and then I lost you, too. You started over again like I didn't even exist. One day you decided, 'I think I'll go get a new life, la dee da.'" She parodied her mother's high-pitched voice and hurled the last words like stones.

They hit their mark. Mimi gasped. "Oh Meghan!" she cried. "I loved you from the minute you were born, and I never stopped. But I needed to follow my own dreams. And I knew you were safe here with your grandpa, he's my dad after all. I knew he was taking good care of you."

She pressed her fingers to her temples. "Can you ever forgive me? Please don't hate me."

Meghan stared at her mother's pale, pained face. They had missed so much time together!

Six years. Almost half Meghan's lifetime.

A wave of anger and sorrow welled in Meghan's stomach and pressed against her heart, squeezing the air out of her lungs. She could barely breathe, her chest and throat blocked by unshed tears.

She swallowed, and gasped in a breath.

And then they came, tears flooded out, like water breaking through a dam. They washed down Meghan's face, soaking her cheeks and flowing down her chin and onto her neck, like a river washing the edges of sharp stones.

"How could I hate you?" Meghan said, sobbing now. "You're my mother."

Mimi's face crumpled in relief. She reached out. Meghan let herself be pulled onto her mother's lap. She curled into a ball, knees to chest, her head nestling under her mother's chin. Sobs shook her like she was caught in a storm, waves crashing on rocks. Wave after wave, uncontrollable now, no way to hold them back. Waves of anger and hurt, washing out with her tears, washing her insides smooth.

Images flashed through her mind: splashing together in the cool mountain stream, laughing in the fields with Grandpa, and two beds side by side, like sisters.

Mimi rocked back and forth, stroking Meghan's hair until her sobs subsided into quiet sniffles. Meghan rested her head against her mother's chest, listening to the steady rhythm of her heartbeat.

"You're almost too big for me to hold." Mimi clasped Meghan tighter and shifted in the chair, trying to find a more comfortable position. Meghan gently pulled away and settled into her own chair.

"I'll be back soon, Christmas at the very latest," her mother said, "and you know you can visit me whenever you like."

"Of course, Mom." Meghan tried to smile, but her lips wouldn't work right.

"Well, I guess that's it then." Mimi smoothed her shirt where Meghan had rumpled it. "You okay, sweetie?"

"I will be, I think." She felt quiet inside, and lighter. She would miss her mom, but it was better now—a little bit anyway. This time it was Meghan's choice.

"I have a few calls to make." Mimi stood and stretched, arching her back. "Now, where did I put my phone?"

Meghan turned her head to answer, but her mother was already walking away.

The garden hummed with the sound of rustling leaves, birds chirped and twittered. Meghan sat with her eyes half closed, absorbing the sounds and scents and colors of the garden while she tried to figure out what she was feeling. She knew what she wasn't feeling—she wasn't mad at her mother anymore.

She would never get back the lost years, or the mother she'd missed for so long, the mother who lived in the house with pink checkered curtains, the mother who painted a castle on the wall and clouds on the ceiling. Mimi hadn't been that person for years. But she did have a mother, a real mother who loved her—never stopped, always would. Not the mother who would settle down and marry Brian, not the mother who would be here all the time. She had to let go of that mother, she didn't exist.

Maybe love was all her real mother could give her. Maybe that was enough.

••

"No more tears, now." Grandpa set a tray on the table and unloaded cups, a teapot, and a bowl of strawberries. He settled into a chair and poured the tea. "You'll make your grandpa cry too." His eyes were swollen—he'd been doing plenty of crying. "Saying goodbye is always hard, but I'm not going anywhere. You can come back anytime you like."

"She wants me to come home with her—"

"Yes, I understand," he said, his voice so low and gravely it was almost a whisper. "A girl needs to be with her mother." Grandpa's jaw quivered. He took a sip of tea.

"She wants me to come home with her," Meghan repeated, "but I'm already home. I belong here, Grandpa. This is my home."

Grandpa sat stunned for a moment, then his face lit with joy and relief. "Thank the dear Lord!" He pushed back his chair and stood to hug her, Meghan held on tight. She breathed in his good, soapy smell, and listened to the thumping song of his heart.

"I thought I was losing you for sure," he said, and kissed the top of her head.

The phone rang faintly from the house. Her mother opened the kitchen door and leaned out, holding her hand over the receiver. "Telephone, Meghan!" she called. "It's a boy. Danny, I think he said his name was."

Meghan's face flushed red.

"Danny, a fine Irish name if ever there was one." Grandpa gave her a little shove. "Go on with you, then."

"Grandpa! He's just a friend."

Grandpa winked at her. "Don't keep the young man waiting."

"Tell him I'll be right there, Mom!" She flapped her wings and took off toward the house.

"It looks like I'm losing you already," Grandpa said. "My little girl is growing up."

But Meghan barely heard him. A sound filled her ears, a strong and steady beat.

It was the sound of her own wings.

# Acknowledgments

When my son was born, I delighted in reading him my favorite children's books . . . before long, my childhood dream of becoming a children's book author bubbled to the surface. Thank you Daniel, for re-awakening that dream, and for your steady, enthusiastic support through every twist and turn of my journey to publication.

Thank you to my wonderful husband, Doug. I appreciate the sacrifices you made when I committed to writing full time. You are my rock. I love you.

There are many people who encouraged me throughout my life. First on that list are my parents, Alvin and Sara Duskin, Allan Lewis, and my amazing mom, Connie Lewis, who was exceptionally brave, creative, wise, and kind. Her spirit is part of every good thing I do. Together my parents filled my life with books, music, and poetry. They introduced me and my siblings to different cultures, inspired compassion for people and concern for our planet, and encouraged us to become our most authentic selves.

Love and thanks to my sisters and brothers for their unwavering support. Special thanks to my sister Laura, who provided feedback on my first picture book drafts and treated my dream of becoming an author with tenderness and respect.

Thank you to my forever friend, Christina Price, who is part of all my stories. I am so grateful for our lifetime friendship! I appreciate your kindness and honesty in critiquing this book's first draft. There is no one else I could have entrusted with that early manifestation of such a fragile dream.

Gratitude and love to Lana Price, who was a second mother to me in Carmel Highlands, and my summer-mother throughout my teens. Your appreciation for art and literature permeated my spirit.

Much love to my friends from Edgewood Avenue. Our childhood experiences are woven into this book: playing freeze tag and hide-and-seek on our block, hanging out after school in Sutro Forest, sharing hopes and secrets . . . growing up together. It was a golden time. Special thanks to Kip deFaria, for reading my favorite journal entries and telling me I should become a writer someday. Thank you Clare Freitas, for your friendship, and for making wings with me out of cardboard and duct tape and running down our hill, trying to fly. You never laughed at me for dreaming.

Heartfelt thanks to Sharon Chriscoe, Jess Shaw, and the wonderful friends and critique partners I have met through the SCBWI Blueboards. I'm grateful for the encouragement, wisdom, and generosity of our amazing community.

Appreciation and love to my friend Amanda Mann, for believing in me, and for encouraging me not to give up.

To my readers: thank you for joining me on this journey! I hope you love *Butterfly Girl* as much as I loved writing it for you.